The Hawk

Under His Wings Trilogy
Book 2

by

Ronna M. Bacon

Dedication

The story of The Hawk, Leith Bradley, is lovingly dedicated to my father, Ronald Bradley Bacon, a carpenter by trade. Some of his actual words to me are contained in the book. As I sit here and contemplate this story, I can hear his words to me, that he so often repeated during the last year of his life, "You did a wonderful job." Dad, for you. Luv you lots and miss you.

Job 39:26
"Is it by your understanding that the hawk soars, Stretching his wings toward the south?

Psalms 61:3
"For You have been a refuge for me, A tower of strength against the enemy.

Proverbs 18:10
The name of the Lord is a strong tower, the righteous run to it and are safe.

Table of Contents

Prologue
Chapter 1
Chapter 2
Chapter 3
Chapter 4
Chapter 5
Chapter 6
Chapter 7
Chapter 8
Chapter 9
Chapter 10
Chapter 11
Chapter 12
Chapter 13
Chapter 14
Chapter 15
Chapter 16
Chapter 17
Chapter 18
Chapter 19
Chapter 20
Chapter 21
Chapter 22
Chapter 23
Epilogue
Dear Readers

Prologue

Moving stealthily, the black form inched his way through the building, searching for the crates he needed. Using the flashlight he carried sparingly, he checked the labels. The crates were there, just as promised. He opened them as quietly as he could, checking around frequently for the security guard. He had no desire to be found.

The packets placed as far down as he could reach, he tapped the lids back on. A noise to his left stopped him and he crouched, clicking off his light. The security guard's large light flashed around and then moved on.

He slipped back out as quickly and as silently as he could. The alarm here was a joke, easy to disarm and easy to arm again. He laughed to himself as he looked around outside the building and then slid easily around the locked gate. The packets would leave the factory tomorrow and then he'd would pick them up once they got where they were headed.

Chapter 1

Leith Bradley slowed his pickup and then turned into the parking lot for Sullivan's Tiles. It was a small family-owned store, a bit more expensive than the larger stores, but he would have to drive further and was not guaranteed the selection they had here. John Sullivan went out of his way to have quality tile, marble, and granite, and had a selection not available in most stores.

Leith parked and then headed into the store. John wasn't out front but Leith knew where the dolly was and soon had found the thin-set, tiles, and grout he wanted. Wheeling the loaded dolly over to the counter, he waited. This was so unlike John. He always was around, hearing the door chime even in the warehouse at the back.

Leith looked around, then stepped behind the counter. Something felt off.

"John, are you here?" he called, walking back into the warehouse. Pallets lined the walkways and shelving was interspersed as well.

"John?" he called again. It was darker here than he expected, darken than usual. Lights seemed to be out.

Leith continued towards the back, not finding anyone around. Then the merest whisper of sound found him. He turned but not quick enough. A hard fist connected with his jaw, sending him backwards and into crates of tiles. His head slammed back and he crumpled to the floor.

The figure, clad in jeans and a hoodie, stood over him. He brought his foot back and kicked Leith in the ribs. Leith lay unmoving, oblivious to the world around him. Blood trickled slowly from the cut on his jaw.

The figure crouched down and then stood. He looked around, not finding what he wanted. The crates were to be here. His contact had told him which ones he needed and they were missing. He cursed, then kicked at Leith again.

Sound from the front of the store brought his head around. His gaze shot through the warehouse and he slipped silently to the door. He would be back.

****

Regan Evans hummed softly to herself as she juggled a cardboard tray of coffees, a bag of muffins, tile catalogues, and her keys. She touched the door and found it unlocked. Guess Uncle John beat me this morning, she thought. He must be feeling better. Regan had returned to her hometown, to help her uncle manage the tile store while her parents had taken a well-deserved month-long vacation. She hadn't heard from them in a couple of days, but she figured she would soon.

Setting the tray of coffees on the counter, she dropped the bag of muffins to answer the phone. This was not her most favourite part of the business—dealing with the customers. She much preferred to be laying the tiles herself. After hanging up the phone, she shrugged out of her jacket and gathered up her purse to take back to the office.

She looked at the loaded dolly and wondered. Uncle John must have been working on an order for a customer.

"Uncle John," she called, "I have your coffee," as she headed back to the office just off the showroom. That's strange, she thought. The door is closed. It's never closed when we're open.

She turned the knob and stepped in. Her purse and coat hit the floor as she dropped down by her uncle. He looked to be asleep. She reached out a shaking hand and felt. Yes, he had a pulse. She trembled as she snagged the phone and called 911.

Soon, the place was filled with police personnel and paramedics. She watched as they worked on her uncle and then loaded the stretcher into the ambulance. She was torn. She felt she needed to stay but needed to go. Ben Johnson nodded at her and sent her with her uncle.

Caleb Logan strode through the door of the store and looked around, keen eyes taking in everything. Ben moved towards him just a shout came from the warehouse area. Caleb and Ben hit the warehouse floor in full run, almost plowing down a young newly recruited officer.

The officer's pale face indicated something else was going on. Caleb shot him a swift glance. First time for a body, he thought. He jerked his head for the officer to go past him.

Ben knelt beside the crumpled body. Feeling for a pulse, he breathed a sigh of relief. "We'll need another ambulance."

"Get us some more light." Caleb crouched beside Ben. "Wonder who we have. Regan didn't think anything was disturbed but she found it strange there was the loaded dolly at the front and no customer."

Ben nodded. "That is strange. I wouldn't think a tile company had much to steal, other than their cash for a day, and I know for a fact John and Joseph do a deposit every night, keeping just enough out for a day's float."

Caleb turned at the noise behind him and then stood to let the paramedics have his place. He stepped away with Ben, discussing possibilities, when the senior paramedic called to him.

"Caleb, can you come here?"

"What do you have?"

"It's Leith Bradley. He's been pretty beaten up."

Caleb stopped, stunned at the development. What was Leith doing back here? He spun on his heel and stared towards the front of the store. That would be his dolly. Leith was a tile setter and almost exclusively used the Sullivan's stock. He turned back.

"How is he?"

"Not great. He's had a pretty good blow to the face and it looks as if his head hit the crates there."

Caleb watched as they worked on his friend and then rushed him out the door. Ben's hand on his shoulder startled him and he looked around.

"Call Liam. Go. I'll work this."

Caleb thanked the older man and pulling out his phone, headed for his vehicle. This was not a call he wanted to make but Leith was alive. He stopped and looked up at the sullen sky, still with drips of the rain/snow mix coming down. This is not how he planned his day.

Worried, he walked into the Emergency Department of their local hospital. Two victims and he had no idea why. He sighed. He just hoped Leith hadn't gotten mixed up in something like his sister, Laycee, had about six months ago. That adventure had almost cost Caleb his brother and Leith and Liam their sister. The accountant who had masterminded the financial fraud was awaiting trial and he hoped she went away for a long time. Adding the murder of her step-son to the charges just might make it happen.

Caleb headed to the registration desk and then back into the examination area.

"Caleb."

He turned. Liam Bradley was headed towards him. No Laycee but he knew that Joshua and Laycee had had plans to spend the day in a nearby town. Joshua had taken a rare day off from his renovation business.

"What happened? How's Leith?"

Caleb stopped his friend with a hand on his shoulder. "I'm headed back there

14

now. He was unconscious when we found him. He looked like he had taken a beating."

Liam's brown eyes bored into Caleb's. "How does a person get beat up at a tile store?"

Caleb stared back. "That's what I want to know and I intend to find out."

Dr. Young stood next to them as they turned. "Liam, you can go back with Leith for now, but we'll be taking him down shortly for some imaging—X-Rays and a possible CT scan."

Liam nodded and then turned to the room where his brother lay.

The two men watched him go, then Caleb spoke, voice controlled and professional.

"How is he, really?"

Dr. Young pulled off his glasses and scrubbed a hand over his eyes. I'm getting too old for working here all night, he thought. "He's still unconscious. He has at least a concussion, a nasty blow to the jaw that needed stitches. The blow to the back of the head is what concerns me. He also looks as if he was kicked in the ribs."

Caleb's head raised. "So, you knock a man out and then kick when he's down? Unbelievable! How is John?"

"He's fine. He's awake. He said he had been feeling faint this morning and figures he passed out. His blood pressure was high and so was his blood sugar. I'll keep him in for a couple of days to sort it all out." Dr. Young hesitated as if to say more, then shook his head. He couldn't breach the confidence his patients had in him keeping their privacy.

Caleb nodded, then watched as Liam stepped back out of the room as they wheeled Leith away.

Liam's shoulders slumped and he leaned against the wall. How was he supposed to be the head of the family and protect them when they kept getting into situations he couldn't control? At least Laycee was out of town today. He would need to call her. He pulled out his phone and turned it over and over.

Caleb stopped beside him and leant against the wall beside him. "You're bearing those burdens again, Liam."

Liam nodded. Without taking his eyes off his phone, he asked, "Who did this and why?"

"Early stages yet, Liam. The crew is still gathering the evidence. We'll sort it out."

Liam snorted. "Sort it out is right." His eyes raised and there was an angry hard look in them. "You'd better before anything else happens to him."

Caleb took the measure of his friend, knowing his anger was not directed at him. "We will. We will. Call your sister." He turned and walked away, heading back out into the fray, but his heart was heavy. What was happening in his town?

Liam sighed, then punched in his sister's speed dial number. At her answer, he could hear the happiness in her voice. He so hated to destroy that. "Laycee, I need you back here. It's Leith." His voice broke and he swallowed the lump in his throat. "He's been hurt pretty bad."

Laycee gasped and then he heard Joshua speaking with her. He knew they would be back without any further questions and without any hesitation. The three Bradley siblings were close and you didn't strike one but you struck all three.

Chapter 2

Regan stood at her uncle's bedside and grasped his hand. "I thought I was going to lose you."

"Not yet, sweetheart. I've got too much living to do." John looked at his niece. "It'll be up to you to run the store, you know. You're capable and I'm only a phone call away. At least for a couple of days. I can work in the office tomorrow or the next day."

Regan gave an unladylike snort at that. "I know I can, I just don't want to. That's not what I expected when I came back home. I know you can and you no doubt will. You need to listen to the doctor."

John smiled. "The Good Lord has a habit of changing our expectations, throwing in those curve balls. We'll get there. Just lock the door and put a note on it if you have to. People in this town understand and I can bet there'll be ladies and gentlemen from the church dropping by just to help out. It's what we do."

Regan nodded. She knew that. That was small town life. She had run from that 10 years ago. She just wasn't used to it any more, having lived in a large city for so many years. She really didn't know if she was that ready to have the town that involved in her life again.

"Go. Find out how our friend, Leith, is. Caleb wouldn't say."

She nodded. "I will. I feel bad that I didn't know he was there."

"How could you? There was the loaded dolly but I could have been gathering an order."

Regan agreed. "It's still not right. Why would someone attack him and in our store?"

"Leave it to Caleb and his men. Now, go. Do what I asked." John paused. "Regan, make sure that order gets over to Leith's job site. It's important."

Regan dropped a kiss on her uncle's cheek, and then turned. She hesitated as if to say something, then moved to the door, leaving her uncle on his own. He leaned back on his pillows, face drawn and pale. He had hidden how he was feeling until she left but he felt rough. He knew his heart was wearing out. He was ready to join his wife, Maggie, in heaven. His mind drifted into well-remembered Bible verses and then into prayer.

****

Liam stood at the foot of his brother's bed, eyes fixed on him. His hands grasped the foot board, warming the cold metal. His mind was racing as he watched, trying to figure it out. Leith had no enemies. He was the one who watched out for everyone, young and old. Leith lay still, not moving even in pain. A dark purple bruise coloured the left side of his face under the white bandage; he had needed four stitches to close the wound. It was the lump on the back of his head that had the physicians worried. He hadn't woken up or moved since he was brought in hours ago. He knew the concerns the physicians didn't voice. He prayed for his brother to awaken as he dropped his head and closed his eyes in exhaustion. Laycee had been there but Joshua had convinced her to go home for a while and sleep. She hadn't wanted to but it said something about the love she shared with Joshua that she let him overrule her natural instinct to stay with her family.

There was a soft tap and the door and it cracked open letting in a narrow band of light. Liam turned and watched as a young woman entered, the light showing auburn hair.

She stepped forward hesitantly. "Dr. Young said it was okay to come. I just wanted to see how he is," as she nodded at the bed.

Liam remained silent, eyes watching carefully. She looked familiar but he couldn't put a name to her face.

Regan stepped forward, as silently as her boots would let her. Liam looked down as he heard the dull thuds. Interesting, he thought, work boots. A pretty lady like that in work boots.

Regan stopped near the end of the bed as Liam turned once more to his vigil. "Here," she said, as she shoved a cup of coffee towards him. "Dr. Young said to bring this to you and that he would be along shortly.

Surprise had Liam's hand going out for the cup. Now what was going on? he wondered.

Regan studied Leith's still form. She remembered him for their school days and to see him like this was disconcerting, especially as he had been hurt on their property.

"Uncle John wanted to know how Leith was. He sent me up."

Liam turned, silent, as he once again studied her and then nodded. "You're John's niece, Joseph and Rebecca's daughter." At her nod, he continued, "I had heard rumours you were back in town to help your uncle. How is he?"

Regan drew in a deep breath. How many more people would remember how she had run? "He's going home tomorrow. The doctors have adjusted his medications. He hadn't been feeling well and that's what happened to him." She grew silent, and then turned. "I am praying for Leith." She turned and almost ran from the room.

Liam watched her leave, surprised at the tears he had seen in her gray eyes. As the door clicked shut behind him, movement from the bed caught his attention. Setting down the coffee cup, he moved to the head of the bed, placing a hand on Leith's shoulder. Leith was moving restlessly now, head turning. His face grimaced with pain, and then his eyes flickered open, not focusing on anything.

"Hey, Leith, come on, wake up, brother." Liam reached for the call button for the nurse as he continued to study his brother's face. Eyes opening and shutting, Leith was rousing. It had been a long day and Liam was exhausted, but the exhaustion was quickly fleeing.

The nurse entered on silent rubber-shod feet and watched for a minute, then moved to check his vitals. She gave Liam a quick smile and nodded. "He's waking up. Dr. Young is still here, he's been in Emergency all day. I'll page him."

Leith's eyes opened once again and he frowned as he struggled to focus. His mouth was dry as he tried to form words. Someone held a straw to his mouth and he greedily sucked in water. "Where am I? What happened?"

"We were hoping you could tell us. Right now you're in the Riverville Hospital." Dr. Young spoke, then examined Leith. "Well, that hard Bradley head is at work again. You have a concussion and will need to take it easy for a few days. We'll see how you are tomorrow." He spoke over his shoulder, "I need to go see some people who may actually be sick."

Liam smiled. Dr. Young and his wife had been good friends with his parents before they lost both of them, one to an accident and one to heart disease.

Leith stared at the door and then at his brother. "What happened?"

Liam sighed and then spoke, "I wish I knew. You were found beat up and unconscious at the Sullivan's. Had you gone there for more tile?"

"I don't remember. If there's where I was found, then I guess I did. I know I needed to get more of the one tile for that tile work in the kitchen on that house. I also needed some of that special grout and thin-set mortar." Leith's eyes slid closed and his breathing deepened.

Liam settled himself in for the night. He was going nowhere. Someone had attacked his brother and he wasn't letting him face them alone.

****

Regan headed for her car. It was late and she needed to be at the store early tomorrow to meet the cleaning crew. She wanted it back up and running right away. She thought about what had happened that day and drew in a shaky breath.

Looking at the sky, she paused as she unlocked her car door. "Thank you, Lord, for protection. Send healing to Uncle John and Leith and help the police to find out who did this and why. Let us never take for granted Your protection."

She spun at a sound near her but saw nothing. Sliding behind the wheel, she locked her doors before starting the motor and leaving.

She didn't see the dark form rise from behind a car two vehicles over from where she had parked or the fists clenched in anger.

The Jester had missed. The King would not be happy. Cursing at his luck, he turned and headed back to the street to his truck. He ignored the ringing phone. He knew who it was and he was not ready to answer. Soon, he would have to. If he only knew who had hired him to find those packets. He had lingered outside Leith Bradley's room and learned he didn't remember much. That was good because if he did he would need to be dealt with.

****

The King stared out the window, hands clenched together behind his back. Things were not going as he expected. His henchman, the Jester, had failed to abduct that girl. At least Leith was still unconscious. He would be dealt with summarily if he ever remembered anything. He had to find those packets. He had promises to keep and those promises were not in his greedy hands. He turned and stormed around the small office, narrowly missing furniture and file folders. Someone had his packets and when he found them, that person would pay and pay handsomely and not with money.

He pulled out the phone he used to called the Jester. No, that idiot had not called back yet. The clock was ticking and soon his time would be over.

Chapter 3

Leith dug his fingers into the side of the bed, fighting to keep his balance through the dizziness and nausea plaguing him. Laycee stood in front of him, hands planted on her hips, and a frown on her face.

"You are not going home," she decided. "You can hardly stay upright as it is."

"Laycee, leave it." Leith squinted up at her. "I'm going. The paperwork is filled out. The doctor said I need to take it easy but I can go home."

"That's not exactly what he said," Liam spoke up. "He said you could go home if you had someone with you for a few days. And definitely no work."

Leith shrugged, trying to hide the flicker of pain that crossed his face. Okay, so he wasn't doing as well as he thought. The headache was intense, intense enough it hurt to open his eyes. He couldn't afford to be off work. He had a deadline for the tiles being done and there was little grace time in it. He would manage. He groaned as Liam helped him into a wheelchair and then pushed him towards the elevator. Yeah, maybe he would take today off.

Liam shook his head as he wound their way to the door and helped Leith up into his truck. Leith leaned back, eyes closed, his face pale and strained. It took a lot out of him, just that move from the hospital. There was no way he would be ready to work again this week and it was only Tuesday. Liam prepared himself for the argument to follow.

Laycee waved as she pulled away from near them. She would be headed to Leith's house and be planning to stay for a long while, if he knew her. Even Joshua couldn't dissuade her.

Liam stole a quick glance at his brother and then concentrated on the drive. He watched his rearview mirror. There was a small, rusted car sticking really close to his bumper. He turned into the pharmacy and stopped; the car had followed him in and parked down the ways. No one exited it. Taking out his phone, he snapped a quick photo of it and tried to get the license, or what part of the license plate he could through the rust.

Leith's breathing was even and quiet. Liam figured he had fallen asleep and would stay that way for the few minutes he was in the pharmacy. Returning quickly, he scanned the parking lot. The car had left, but he had a bad feeling. Pulling out his phone he sent a quick text with the pictures to Caleb and to Ben. There, it was done— they would look into it.

"Wake up, buddy." Liam carefully shook Leith's shoulder as he stood at the open truck door. Leith stirred but didn't open his eyes. "You're home, Leith. Time to rise and shine."

"Go away. I want to sleep."

Liam grinned, then nudged Leith again. "That you may wish, brother, but if you want to sleep I think a bed might be a bit more comfortable than my truck."

Leith looked around with blurring eyes, then accepted Liam's help to enter his home. He dropped on his couch, put his feet up and dropped out of the world again. Laycee came up beside Liam and wrapped an arm around him as they stood staring at their brother.

"What happened to him, Liam?"

Liam hesitated, then spoke. "Caleb has some ideas but he hasn't said much yet. I think Leith was in the wrong spot at the wrong time. You're staying for a while?"

Laycee nodded.

Liam hugged her, dropped a kiss on her hair, and then headed for the door. "I'll be back around 5 or so. I'll stay the night."

"Thanks, Liam. I'll have supper ready. I'm just glad I can work from home now. Heading up that therapy group is a lot of work but it gives me the most flexibility of us all."

Laycee locked the door, then grabbing a blanket from the closet, draped it over her brother. She undid his sneakers and pulled them off. Liam hadn't bothered with Leith's jacket, so she didn't have to worry about that. She dropped into the easy chair across from him and studied him. Tears were near the surface at the thought that Leith could easily have died. Her anguish turned to prayers and she felt herself calming back down.

****

Regan pulled folders from the supply cupboard and headed back to the counter at the front. Uncle John was right—people from the church had shown up, cleaned up the place and even now a couple of the men his age were working away in the back. The place was tidy, clean and everything that had a place was in its place. She hesitated as she saw a woman leaning on the counter looking out the front.

"Can I help you?"

The woman turned, a big smile on her face. "No, I've come to help you. I'm Hannah Logan, Caleb's wife."

Regan frowned. "I don't know what you can help me with, but go ahead."

Hannah laughed. "Your parents talked a lot about you and how proud they were of you." Regan stared at her, not believing her. "They maintained that you could lay tile with the best of them, that you had apprenticed and were working for a

33

company that did renovations of older homes that needed precise tiling done. So, here's the thing. I'm really good at sales and people stuff. You need help here. You're really good at tiling. Leith will need more help than he's willing to accept. This is what I propose: I work here and you go work for Leith."

Regan's eyes never left Hannah's face. Just where did she come up with that? And how on earth did she ever figure Leith would let her anywhere near the place he was working?

"I think that is a very sound idea." Uncle John spoke from behind her. "Leith can use the help and I know you are just as finicky as he is."

"Uncle John, that's not nice." Regan spun around to take him on, then noticed her cousin, David, hovering behind him. Cousins or not, she had never liked nor trusted him. His scruffy appearance didn't win her over now either. He only came around when he wanted something or needed something.

"Yes, it is. And starting tomorrow, I'm sending you over to his job site. He's shown me the plans. You can handle it."

"Yeah, and who will handle him, or for that matter, you?" Chin tilted, Regan tried her best to stare him down but knew it was a losing battle.

"Liam will." Her uncle grinned at her, knowing she was giving in. "I've seen your work. I've seen his work. Your styles are so close, it's scary. That is rare in this business. Pietro trained you both well."

Regan stared at her uncle. "Pietro trained him?"

Her uncle nodded as Hannah spoke up behind her. "I know Laycee and Joshua will help as will Caleb. Go. You'll enjoy working on that house."

A movement from her cousin caught her eye. Slanting a glance at him, she shuddered. A look of evil had crossed his face and just as quickly disappeared. What was it?

Her eyes moved back and forth between her uncle and Hannah. Now she placed Hannah, a woman slightly older than herself but who had been in clubs at school with her. She sighed. She really did miss the feel of the tiles and the thin-set mortar and the grout, the feeling of pride in laying the tiles and finishing off the pattern. She wasn't all that happy in the store, even though she did love the customers and could put up with answering questions and sharing her knowledge.

"All right, I give." A quick smile from Hannah and a hug from her uncle showed she had made the right decision. "Now, how do I get into the house?"

"I have the keys." A male voice brought her head up. Liam now stood by Hannah.

"Now that's a set-up if I ever saw one!" Regan exclaimed.

"Yes, I guess you could say it was. Why don't we head over to the house and I can show you what Leith has been working on."

Once in the truck, Regan shot Liam a glance. "How is Leith? And bigger question, how is he going to take this?"

"He was sleeping when I left him at home this morning. Yes, he insisted on going home. Laycee's with him. She can work flexible hours so it helps. No matter what he says, he will not be ready to work the heavy full days that he has been lately. He did say he needed to hire but he didn't know of anyone in town who was trained and he didn't have the time to train." Liam looked over at Regan. She was staring out the side window, a shuttered look on her face. "I don't know why you left all those years ago, but I do know that God has brought you back here for just this time. John and your Dad have often spoken, with pride I might add, about your work. You're a natural."

Regan was silent. "I can't talk about why I left. Others are involved. I just had to get away. I just don't like going behind Leith's back" She stopped speaking. "I miss that work. Dad wasn't happy at first that I moved away and had gone into a construction-type of work. He didn't want me working on jobs with the rough and tough men of construction, but Pietro was good. He made sure I was never alone. He treated me like a granddaughter. His sons and grandsons just opened their homes to me. I miss them." She blinked away tears, then looked at Liam. "One thing—if Leith strongly objects, I'm out of there. I won't be put in the middle of a family fight over this."

Liam smiled. Lord, I just think You brought Leith a real friend that he needs. She won't take his nonsense. He needs that.

"I'll handle him. Right now, he's not moving well at all. Dr. Young wants him off work to heal. But he's stressed about this job. He's been behind waiting on the tile and now that he has some of them, he said it would take about a month to finish. I don't understand the tile trade. Ask me about gardens or landscaping, I can help you with that."

Regan looked at him in silence, then turned to stare at the house where Liam had stopped. She knew this house, has loved it since she was a child. It was over one hundred years old she knew, with porches and gingerbread and all the architectural details that fit the age and style. She had never been inside but had always wanted to. It had been the second home for a prominent doctor from Oak City and had recently been sold. She was going to enjoy working here, that is, provided Leith let her.

Liam stood beside his truck, keys in hand, watching Regan's face. He knew they had made the right decision in asking her to help. Now he had to convince Leith that it would work. And he wasn't all that confident he could.

Regan wandered through the house, just enjoying the renovations that were happening, taking the look of the house back to when it was built. The renovator was a master craftsman, she could tell, who loved his work. She looked down at the marble in the main foyer and then made her way through to the kitchen. Here, work was still in progress. She reached out to touch the colourful backsplash. The mixture of colours was true to the palette of one hundred years ago. Tiles from outside the country, she knew from what she had been told. The work was precise and very detailed. She looked down at the plans Leith had laying on the covered countertops. Yes, it was very detailed, but she knew she could handle it. She could see Pietro's influence there.

She turned to Liam and nodded. He breathed a sigh of relief, came over and hugged her.

Surprised, she stepped back, looking up at him in shock.

"You'll do," Liam said. "Now I have to beard the lion in his den."

"Can you get me a set of keys and take me back to my truck? Seeing as Hannah has kicked me out, I'll start today."

"That I can do." And thank you, Lord, Liam breathed a small sigh of relief.

"Who's the renovator, Liam? He's doing good work."

Liam stopped in surprise. "It's Joshua Logan, Caleb's brother. He has a real talent for fixing up these older homes."

Regan nodded. "He always was interested in that."

Chapter 4

Ben knocked and then entered Caleb's office. He dropped down in the chair in front of the desk, a discouraged look on his face. This was unusual for Ben.

"What do you have?" Caleb studied the older officer. He could see the fatigue in his face. Ben had been working hard to try and find the culprits of the break-in but he had run out of leads.

"Nothing. There was no evidence that the team could find. I just don't know, Caleb. Something is there." Running his hand through his gray hair, he continued, "It's not like other break-ins we have had. Nothing was taken. No property damage done. If Leith hadn't been there at the wrong time, he wouldn't have been hurt. Something smells, though. Just like last time. This isn't the first time John has mentioned someone searching their warehouse."

Caleb leaned back in his chair. "I know. There's something there." He leaned forward again and resting his elbows on his desk, he said, "Get the information from John about their suppliers. Maybe there's a link there somewhere we don't know about."

Ben's keen eyes looked up and studied Caleb. "You're thinking smuggling or something along that line?"

Caleb hesitated, then nodded. "And don't tell me that hasn't crossed your mind. We have a lot of leg work to do."

Ben snorted. "You mean I do. I hear John's niece is going to be working with Leith. How's that going?"

Caleb shook his head. It was amazing to him how Ben knew his town and what was happening. Over the years, he had formed a link of friends and contacts who shared information with him. He laughed. "Liam was breaking the news. I'm glad it's not me. Hannah is going to help out in the store while the boys are at preschool. I'm okay with that. We just need to find the culprit."

"And with that being said, I'll just toddle off and see what I can find out." Ben shut the door behind him.

Caleb sat in deep thought. What was happening in his town? First the accountant with her financial schemes and murders and now this. Was it just that Leith was in the wrong place at the wrong time? Was is just a simple break-in or as he suspected something much deeper and more sinister? He would let Ben puzzle it out for a while. Ben loved digging into these mysteries. Caleb knew he wouldn't rest until he came to the right conclusion, whatever that might be.

****

The Jester finally answered the King's call.

"What happened? Why did you attack Leith? You have brought attention to us that shouldn't be."

The Jester could feel the fury vibrating through the phone.

"He saw me. He was right where the crates were supposed to be."

"You idiot!   Now the police are involved. They won't stop looking. You have may just blown up something I have had going for a long time. Handle it."

The Jester winced as the called ended in an abrupt manner. Yes, he would have to handle it.   That Innocent had been wrong. He had given him the wrong information. He would track him down and he would pay. Then he would have to find those crates and those packets.   His own life very likely depended on that fact.   He ran his hand through his shortly cropped light brown hair. He had a sudden thought.   If he could get close to Regan, maybe she could lead him to the crates. His face brightened. It wouldn't be a hardship getting to know this beautiful lady.

****

Leith stirred, grimacing at the pain in his head at the movement. His eyes opened, shut and then openly slowly again as he adjusted to the light. He heard movement in front of him and saw Laycee sitting on the edge of her chair across from him, head tilted to the side so she could look at him.

"How's the head?"

"How do you think it is? It hurts."

Laycee gave a soft laugh. "Of course it does, brother, of course it does. You have a concussion. Now, do you want something to drink or eat?"

Leith laid there, then slowly sat up, fighting the spinning of the room and the nausea. He did feel better upright. Now he just needed to make his way for a shower and he might feel more human. As his hands rubbed his face, he added a shave to that. His fingers stopped at the bandage and he fingered it.

"You had four stitches there in case you forgot."

"Like I remember that."

Laycee laughed again. "The ladies will love your battle scars, you know."

Leith whipped a pillow at her, then regretted it. Laycee's face crunched up as she shared his pain. A movement to his side showed Joshua coming in from the kitchen, Liam on his heels.

"Good to see you upright," Joshua said, as he perched on the chair arm beside Laycee.

Leith squinted at them, then moved to stand. He was shaky. He felt like he had been run over and tossed out with the trash. Not a good feeling. The dizziness and nausea were there but not as bad as they had been when he stood in the hospital room. What day was it any way?

"It's Thursday," Liam commented. Leith glared at him. "I knew you would want to know. Now let's get you looking more human. I'm glad you put in that guest suite downstairs. You won't be climbing stairs for a while."

Leith stopped once he entered the bathroom and stared at his reflection. He looked as bad as he felt. Maybe the shower and shave would help.

Liam propped a shoulder against the door frame and watched his brother, frown in place. Their eyes met in the mirror. They would talk soon and not in front of Laycee if they could help it. She would want to know every detail of what happened and would go charging in to try and help. Leith did not want that. Not knowing what or who was horrible.

"We'll talk once Laycee goes home. Are you going to manage okay?"

Leith looked around and sighed. "I think so. No tub side to crawl over so that helps. Just stick around close in case I need help."

Liam nodded, closing the door to the room. He wandered over to the window and moved the blind slats to look out. The guest room faced the side street. His gaze took in everything, then stopped. There was that rusted car again. Who was it? He made a note to call Caleb or Ben. Someone was following one of them and he wanted to know who.

Leith stepped from the bathroom, looking much more like himself, but still shaky. He sat on the bed as Liam approached. Looking up, he asked, "Has Laycee gone?"

Liam nodded. "Joshua took her home. She left some soup and fresh bread. Feel like something to eat?"

"Yeah, I think so. Just give me a minute. This feels worse than when I took that hit playing football in high school."

"It was worse, much worse. Someone tried to kill you." Leith's eyes flew to his brother's. "Come on. Let's get some food into you and I'll tell you what's been happening."

An hour later, Leith was back on the couch, coffee mug in hand. He looked around the room. It was bare. It needed something but he had no idea what. He should think about a dog, he thought, but with his work so busy and putting in so many hours, it wouldn't be fair. He really needed to try and find someone to hire. Maybe Pietro would have a lead on someone he had trained who was looking for a move to a smaller town. He would call him in the next couple of days and asked. He really didn't know how he was going to finish the Bell House job.

Liam had finished cleaning the kitchen and sat in one of the recliners while Leith was lost in thought. He watched his brother carefully, noting that he was not as cautious in his movement, but he could tell the headache was still there. He stood and went to find some painkillers. He handed them to Leith. Leith took them without comment so Liam knew he was hurting. Sitting back down, he sipped at his own coffee and waited. He had great patience, but Leith had even more. It was sometimes a competition between the two as to who gave in first.

"Okay, Liam. Tell me. I don't remember anything from that morning. The night before I had made plans to go get more supplies. You tell me it looks as if I did. Fill me in."

Liam looked at his hands. He sighed, set his coffee mug on the table beside him and then leaned forward. "What I am telling you is what Caleb and Ben have deduced. You had gone to the store, not found anyone out front and loaded up your dolly. You went looking for John and happened on a thief. He knocked you out. When he hit you, you slammed back into some crates and that's how you ended up with the concussion. John's niece came in, found him and then left with the ambulance to take him to the hospital. Officers were searching the warehouse and found you. The young officer that found you—he thought you were dead. It was not a pretty scene for him. They didn't realize at first it was you."

Leith shuddered. He didn't remember but maybe it was a good thing. "So what happened with John?

"I guess he hadn't been feeling well and passed out. He's back at work."

"Work." Leith grimaced. "I need to get back there tomorrow. There's that timeline I need to meet. Other trades are depending on me finishing when scheduled."

Liam shook his head. "You're not ready."

"I don't have a choice. There's only me."

"Then maybe it's time you found someone to hire."

Leith looked at his brother, and thought that he had read his mind. "I know. I just don't have the time to interview and hire. It's not like hiring a labourer. This is detailed work that needs skilled hands."

Liam looked at his brother and then his gaze looked past him. Leith's eyes narrowed. Yes, he thought. Liam has done something and just doesn't know how to tell me.

"What did you do?"

Liam looked guilty. "John knew of someone Pietro trained that was in the area on a temporary basis. He says he's seen this person's work and he found it really hard to tell it from yours. I spoke with Pietro. This person has been highly trained by him and was working with him up until about six weeks ago before asking for a temporary leave of absence to come back to this area."

"Liam, why? Why? Why go behind my back?" Leith stood and paced.

"Leith, stop and think about it. You're not able to. You have said that Pietro is the best, that you would willingly hire anyone he trained. We'll go over tomorrow and see. If you don't like it, then I will personally tear out the work done and redo it under your supervision."

Leith was frustrated and hurting. He bit his tongue before he said something he would regret. Finally, he gave a short nod and sat back down. His head dropped on the back of the couch.

"I'm frustrated." He stated the obvious. "Why did this happen?"

Liam watched his brother, assessing his mood. "I don't know, Leith. I don't have the answers for you. I have watched you over the years. You are the watcher in our family. You watch over us all and step in without a word. Someone like that has difficulty asking or accepting help." He paused, then continued, "When I look at you, I think of how God has provided a strong tower for us to run to and be safe. You are like a hawk perched on that tower, watchful and ready. It is time you yourself run for that tower."

Leith's body movements stilled as he thought over his brother's words. Liam had him pegged. Liam knew both he and Laycee well. Laycee was really like the sparrow—she had had a poor self image for years until she went through all the stuff last year and realized that God really did count her more important than this lowly bird.

He sighed, and raised his head to look across the room. Liam's eyes were closed and Leith knew he was in prayer. He cleared his throat and Liam's eyes opened.

Leith said nothing, just rose from the couch, and stopped beside his brother. He hesitated, then gripped his brother's shoulder, and made his way to his bedroom. He needed sleep if he was to work tomorrow.

****

The Jester watched the lights go out at Leith's home. He waited. He would probably need to find another vehicle. If they got sight of this one, they would remember it. He keyed the vehicle to life and headed out. Small towns were good but they could be bad too. He headed for a larger town and drifted around, looking at the malls and bars. He finally found what he wanted. He ditched the rusted vehicle he had been driving and slipped behind the wheel of the nice new extended cab pickup. Now he had height, muscle and metal. He would win this fight.

Driving back to his home, he parked where the vehicle could not catch any eyes and headed for bed. Tomorrow would be here soon, and he needed to search. If only the Innocent had not screwed up. He would have to be dealt with and would once the Jester had what the King wanted. He wondered what was in the packets. Maybe

he would take a peek if he could get a
chance.

Chapter 5

Leith struggled the next morning. The headache was better but his body was aching all over. He dressed and slowly climbed down the stairs. He could hear Liam moving around in the kitchen and headed that way. Liam turned to look at him and then handed him his painkillers. Leith shook his head but Liam's hand shoved the bottle back. Glaring at him, he snatched the bottle and downed the medication.

"I'm sorry, Liam. That was uncalled for."

"No problems. Let's head for SueEllen's for breakfast. You need food."

Leith gave a small laugh. Yes, he definitely felt like eating.

At the local cafe they liked, Leith held the door for a young woman exiting. She glanced up and gave a word of thanks, gray eyes widening slightly when she saw him.

Auburn hair was caught back in a pony tail under a baseball cap. Leith smiled, then frowned. He should know her. He watched her walk away, then entered at a push from behind. Liam had been standing there. Liam snickered. He had recognized Regan.

"There's Caleb. Let's join him." Liam lifted a hand to SueEllen and she nodded. Their usual breakfast would be on the way.

Sliding into chairs at Caleb's table, they greeted one another as mugs of coffee were set in front of them.

Once their meals had arrived and they had each asked the blessing on their food, Leith looked at Caleb.

"Tell me what you have. Who did this?"

Caleb's hand hesitated as he raised a forkful of eggs to his mouth. He chewed and then swallowed. Wiping his mouth, he sought for words. "We don't have a lot, Leith. There was not a lot of evidence there."

Leith's mouth hardened into a straight line. "Break-ins don't happen at tile stores.

Other than the day's receipts, they don't have material that someone can easily haul away and sell on the black market." He worked his way through his breakfast, the food helping to clear the fog he was working under.

Liam's eyes travelled between his brother and his friend. There was something that was going on and it was causing undercurrents there. He hesitated to speak but he knew he had to.

"Where does John and Joseph get their supplies from? Is there something in one of the shipments that someone was looking for?"

Leith's eyes shot to him, shocked at the thought. Smuggling? No way. John and Joseph wouldn't be involved in that.

Caleb reached for his mug, took a swallow, and then looked around the cafe. There were no customers close enough to hear what he was about to say.

He still hesitated. The investigation was still in early stages and he didn't have a lot he could share at the moment. He finally nodded and looked at his two friends.

"That's what we're thinking." He raised a hand as Leith opened his mouth to speak. "We don't suspect either John or Joseph. They're not the ones we're focusing on. We have to trace the shipments back to the factory and then follow them to here. It's not a quick process. We are working with authorities in other countries. We will also likely have to involve federal authorities here in this country if contraband has crossed the border. Be patient." He stopped and pulled out his cell phone. "I need to go. Are we still on for dinner on Sunday?"

Liam nodded, then looked at Leith. "I am. I don't know about him though."

Leith punched his brother in the arm, then regretted at the discomfort moving through his body. He hauled his body up and headed for the door, knowing Liam had stopped to pay for their meals.

Liam parked before the house. He turned off the ignition, then reached across the cab and caught Leith's arm. "Before you go in, Leith, listen for a minute. I'm sorry. I should have waited and asked you. I know it's your business and I interfered. I shouldn't have. But I really do think you'll be happy. Before you blow it off, listen and look. I was here yesterday and saw the work. It's really good."

Leith stared out the windshield, thinking about his brother had said. They were close and Liam knew him well. He would listen and look but the final decision would be his. He gave a short nod, then shoved open the truck door. He stood for a minute to get his balance. A truck parked in the driveway caught his attention, a little green Ford Ranger. A memory tugged at him but he couldn't draw it to the foreground of his mind. Someone he knew had always wanted a truck like that. He shrugged. It would come.

He stared up at the house. This house had taken a lot from him but had taught him to reach inside, to grow, to expand. He figured part of that was learning to trust others but more so to put his trust fully in God. That was the tough part.

He headed up the walk and the front steps. It had dried so he could step in with his boots on. He noticed that craft paper had been laid over the tile for protection. He hadn't done that, so the new tile setter must have. Strange. Most guys wouldn't think to do that.

He found his way back to the kitchen and stopped. The kitchen was cleaned and as ready to be cooked in as he had ever found a kitchen, minus the appliances. His gaze went around. The floor was finished. He stepped over to the counter and looked. The backsplash was also finished. He reached out and touched it. He loved the colours and the way they played of the light oak cabinets and the off-white countertop. He looked closer at the backsplash, looking for issues, mistakes, anything that stood out. There was nothing. What Pietro had told Liam was the truth. This guy was good. He had doubted but okay, now he was convinced.

He turned to find Liam still standing in the foyer, fingering his keys. Leith stalked over to him and stood in silence. He saw small smile playing around Liam's mouth before he looked up.

"Okay, you were right. This guy's good. Now I have to find him and tell him he has a job."

Liam still had that bit of a smirk on his face. He nodded at the stairs. Liam looked, groaned and knew he had to walk up them, sore body or not.

Stepping onto the floor in the upper hall, he noted the house was almost completed trimmed out, painted, and wallpaper up. Just maybe Joshua would make his deadline. He was doing his best to help his friend. They had had just a few months to do the complete renovation and they were pushing to finish. There was not a lot left but it was time consuming work.

Liam could hear soft humming from ahead of him. He tilted his head. That didn't sound like a man's voice. He listened again. No, definitely female. He looked behind him for Liam. Not there. Traitor, he thought.

He followed the humming down the hall to the master suite and then through it to the open bathroom doorway. He stopped. A slim figure was crouched in the shower, working her way up the wall with the tile, preciseness in every movement. He tilted his head and watched. She was good. He took a look at the worker again—auburn hair, plaid shirt, jeans. She was the woman from the cafe. He still felt he knew her but his mind was not functioning well today and he couldn't put a name to her. He waited until she sat back on her heels and then cleared his throat.

Regan closed her eyes. Leith was here. Well, it had been fun while it lasted. She mentally prepared herself to go back to selling tiles in the tile store. She turned and looked up at him.

Leith studied her. He still couldn't place her but he knew her.

"You're good. Liam said Pietro trained you."

"He did. I worked for him for years until I came back here."

Leith moved closer to the large shower area. She must have started early today, a lot of tile was laid already. She would pretty much be finished with the tiling by tomorrow and then would be doing the grouting.

He looked down at her upturned face. "Want a job? I'm hiring. I have more work than I can really manage on my own." He watched as her eyes slid closed and then opened again.

"If you really mean that, then yes." She stood and offered him her hand.

"We can do the paperwork later. Come with me. I need to go let Liam gloat and say I told you so. I just need your name to start with."

She stared at him. He really didn't know. "It's Regan Evans."

Leith spun from where he was walking ahead of her and stepped back to stop in front of her, causing her to take a step backwards. "That's why I know you. Regan. I often wondered where you were. Your parents and uncle sometimes spoke of you but never where you were working. Welcome home."

Regan stared up at him, shaken at his response. Being welcomed back into her hometown was not what she had expected. But then again, not many people knew why she had left, not even her parents. That was a secret she hadn't shared with them, but sighing inside, she knew she would have to.

She followed Leith down the stairs to where Liam was standing. Liam smiled and held out a hand to welcome her. She smiled back. Just maybe this was going to work out after all.

Liam left and Leith turned to Regan, motioning her to the kitchen. She trailed after him, not knowing what he was going to say, even though he had told her he was hired. She stopped in the door.

Leith stood leaning against the counter and spoke. "Come here, Regan." As she moved forward, he spoke, "You're very good. I can't really tell where you left off or I did. That is great. Thank you."

Regan breathed a sigh of relief and then nodded. "I need to get back to the tiles upstairs. Anything else?"

He shook his head. "Just make sure you leave by 5 tonight. It's Friday. We shut down by 5 and don't work the weekends. We need those breaks."

She was surprised, knowing he was pushing, but agreed.

****

The Jester said in his stolen truck across from the house and waited. How long would it be before they left and he could follow them?

The flash of lights in his mirror startled him. A police cruiser was headed down the street. He pulled away from the curb, taking care not to draw attention to himself. Someone might have reported him. As he turned a corner, he breathed a sigh of relief. No, not spotted. It must just be a routine patrol. He would be back. First, he had to find the Innocent. He was hiding but he would be found.

Chapter 6

Leith sank back into Laycee's couch. It was comfortable. He rubbed a hand along the leather. It was not what he had expected her to get after her furniture had been destroyed in the break-in last fall, but he could see Joshua's hand in that. He was good for his sister. He sank his head back and closed his eyes, starting as he felt a warm body crawl into his lap. He looked down - Defiant, Laycee's sheltie, had decided he needed to be comforted. He rubbed the black and tan fur on the dog, then the white ruff. Defiant leaned harder into him, content, the reached up to lick at the wound on his jaw.

Leith pushed his head away, telling him it was healing and he didn't need his licking to help.

Hannah Logan sat down at the other end of the couch. He slanted a look at her and saw her smile. "How much trouble am I in?" She asked, eyes sparkling with mirth.

"Plenty. I'm going to tell the police on you." She laughed. "Actually, I need to say thank you. You pushed as did Liam. Regan is really good. I hope she'll stay around."

"Good. I'm glad that worked out. She was a really great kid, and I suspect has turned into a wonderful young lady."

"You knew her well from before?"

Hannah shook her head. "We were in some of the same clubs, but she really didn't let anyone close. Then as soon as she graduated, she took off. No one ever said why. Maybe she'll open up with you."

Leith shook his head. "No. Not interested, Hannah."

Hannah laughed. "We'll see. But there is something I should warn you about. I have talked to Caleb and he said to let you in on it. Regan's cousin, David, is back. I caught some looks and undertones between the two of them the other day. It wasn't pleasant. David's look was that typical if looks could kill, you'd be dead look. John hasn't said much, but I get the impression he's not happy with David."

Leith thought about her words. "Thanks. I wouldn't pry but I'll see if she says anything. If you hear anything, let me know."

"I will." Hannah laid her hand on his arm. "I am so glad you're getting better. I was really scared when I heard."

Leith smiled as she arose and went to find her sons. He stood and then moved to the door. It was time he left. Tomorrow would be here soon and it would be a long day.

****

Regan muttered to herself as she drove to the job site. Why had she let them talk her into this? She knew better. She had had a crush on Leith Bradley all during high school. Now she had to keep herself in line so he didn't guess she still liked him. Maybe he would work in another part of the house all day and they won't cross paths. Yeah, right, like that will happen, she murmured. As she stopped in the driveway, Leith's truck was already there. She was surprised he was driving but then again, he wouldn't let anyone smother him with care. That was not him.

She grabbed her knapsack out of the truck and the kit she used to carry her tools. Pietro had given her some and she had accumulated the rest over the years. She headed for the door and heard her name called. She turned to see Leith striding across the driveway, headed for her. He reached for her kit and took it. Surprise had her releasing it. That was something they were going to have to talk about. She carried her own weight and that meant her own kit.

"Good morning." Leith smiled at her. "I've been inside. I see you finished the tiling in the bathroom. You came back on the weekend!" He accused.

She shrugged. "It needed to be done. We were down two or three days. Today I can finish it and move on."

Leith held the door for her and then stopped her with a hand on her arm. "I meant what I said, Regan. Work stops at 5 on Fridays and doesn't get picked up again until Mondays. In this job, we need that break. You have to learn to pace yourself. I know Pietro worked all kinds of hours but I don't. I have other things outside of work to do."

She looked down at her feet. She had been wrong, no matter how much she had wanted to please him. "I'm sorry. I'll remember." She grabbed her kit and climbed the stairs. Today had gotten off to a bad start and it was her fault.

Leith watched her climb the steps. He ran a hand through his black hair and frowned. That didn't go as he had planned. He would talk to her again at lunch.

Leith appeared at the doorway of one of the guest suites four hours later. "Regan, it's lunch time. Come on down to the kitchen."

"Be there shortly."

Leith headed back to the kitchen. He had found out from John what Regan's favourite meal was at the cafe and had talked SueEllen into doing up take out for him. She didn't often do a take out order but she liked both Regan and him. Secretly, she wanted to help along a romance and thought they were suited to each other.

Regan appeared in the doorway, nose twitching. Leith had set up a small folding table and brought in some folding chairs. He looked up at her.

"I dislike sitting on the floor to eat. There are part of the tools of my trade." He had spread out their meal and it smelled wonderful. "I needed to apologize to you. Thought lunch would help."

Regan's fingers went to her lips and her eyes brimmed with laughter. She tried hard but the snicker would out. "You told SueEllen you had to eat some crow. This is what she provided?"

Leith looked down at the fried chicken dinners and laughed. "I'd rather eat chicken than crow. Come on and sit."

They were about half-way through their meal when Leith stopped and wiped his mouth and then his fingers on the paper napkin. He gathered his thoughts and then spoke, "I did you a disservice, Regan. As a man in construction, I dislike seeing women working in the trades." He held up his hand as she went to speak. "Please, let me finish. Not all job sites are great. In fact, most of them have rough and tumble men on them who are not pleasant to women. There's a lot of talk and such that goes on that I wouldn't want a woman exposed to. Besides, it can be really heavy work and a woman's body is put together different from a man's. Women aren't meant to do the heavy work a man is—they're not built that way. It is hard enough on a man's body. Having said that, I know how Pietro and his family protected you. That's how it will be with me. I'll pull you off a job if I think you need to be pulled off from it, and please don't protest against it. A lot of the time we're on our own or there are a few others working on site. I like working on Joshua's renovations. He has a really good clean crew working for him. He has also chosen well the sub-contractors he hires. I know you would be okay around them."

"Thank you, Leith. I will be my best." She pushed her meal container aside and propped her chin in her hands. "How long do you figure for this job, and what do you have coming up next?"

Talk went to the tiling work that was going on. Leith liked the input that Regan offered. She did have some good ideas.

Later that day, Regan started down the stairs. She heard muffled noise from the back and headed that way. She needed to talk to Leith about an issue that had come up.

She stepped through the kitchen to the back porch where Leith had stored the tiles. A black form spun at she stepped through and charged at her, knocking her back against the door. She screamed and the intruder disappeared out the back door.

Leith slammed his truck into park at the sight of a black figure racing around from the back of the house. He jumped from his vehicle but his body was too beaten up at this point to chase. Pulling out his phone, he called the emergency services and then ran for the house. Regan. Was she okay? He took the stairs two at a time and searched the upstairs, opening closets and doors. She wasn't there.

He called for her as he sped back down the stairs and thought he heard a voice from the kitchen. Reaching the kitchen, he saw Regan on her feet, leaning against the wall, hand on her back. He stopped in front of her.

"Are you okay?" He led her to a chair and pushed her down, noting her grimace as he did so.

She nodded. "Just had the wind knocked out of me." She took a deep breath. "Who was that?"

Leith shook his head. " I don't know. I couldn't chase but the police are on their way. Where was he?"

"In the back, at the crates of tiles. I came looking for you and found him instead." She stood and headed to the back porch. "What was he after?"

Leith's hand came out and he stopped her. "No, we can't go out there. We have to leave it. I guess it's now what you call a crime scene."

Regan's eyes slid shut. He was right. Another crime scene. What was this guy after or who was he after?

****

Ben found them an hour later. Regan had returned to her work in the upstairs. Leith had hovered for a while, then gone to see what was happening in the back porch. He had returned shortly before Ben came up the stairs and had pulled Regan from her work, telling her to wrap it up for the day. Regan had gone to stand at the window, watching the activity below, Leith standing in the middle of the room, hand on his head, lost in thought.

"Leith, Regan." Ben spoke from the doorway. Both turned at the sound of his voice. "We need you to come down stairs for a minute." At the sober look on his face, they exchanged glances, then followed him down the stairs.

Caleb stood at the kitchen counter, notebook out as he scrawled in it. He glanced up, then added more details to what he was writing. He stopped, leaning both hands on the counter. Looking up, he stared at them. Leith stared back, but Regan dropped her eyes.

Caleb nodded to the doorway and led them out to the back porch. Crates of the tiles were broken open, with some of the tiles shattered. Leith groaned. He didn't need this. He was so close to finishing. He prayed he had enough tile so that he could actually finish on time.

Ben spoke from behind them. "We think it was the same one who broke into the store. There's not a lot of evidence. Did you see his face, Regan?"

"No. All I saw was a black form coming at me. He had on a hoodie that blocked most of his face but I really didn't get a chance to see even that. It was just too fast." She stopped, remembering something. "I did see something. A tattoo or birth mark or something on a hand."

Caleb and Ben exchanged glances. "Which one?"

Regan held both of her hands out in front of her, frowning. She spun to face the doorway and held her hands up as if to push at someone. "The left one. On the inside of the wrist. Black and green and some blue, I think. I really don't know what the shape was, though. It's just kind of mingled together."

Caleb nodded. "That's more than what we had before. If you remember anything more, let me know. Now, to the crates. Leith, were they all opened?"

Leith shook his head. "No, we only open them as we need to, unless there is a great mismatch in colour. These ones have been great. I haven't had to open any more one or two at a time." He looked around at the opened crates and destruction. "What was he looking for?"

Caleb and Ben were silent. Leith looked at them. "All right, give. You have suspicions. This now involves me more than just being in the wrong place at the wrong time."

Ben spoke, "We suspect there has been contraband of some kind shipping from the factory or inserted into the crates at some stage on the delivery route. We have had rumours of this for a while, but nothing concrete that we can fix on. That has changed."

Regan drew in a sharp breath. "You don't suspect my Dad or Uncle, do you? They would never do that."

Caleb shook his head. "No, we don't. We think that the break-ins and missing material your uncle has been tracking are what has held the contraband. We don't know yet what it is." His keen glance speared both of them with a stern look. "We need you to both be very careful. You have had contact with the thief. If they suspect you can identify them, they may come looking for you." He ran a hand through his hair and continued, "We need you to keep on as you have been. Don't let them suspect."

Leith looked at Regan, seeing the whiteness and fear on her face. It seemed more than just what Caleb had said. He would find time to talk with her at some point.

****

The King was once again furious. The Jester had once again failed to find the packets. Just how hard was that task? He would need to be looking for new help or else he would need to pack up and move, and he wasn't about to do that. He had a nice little business going here—the contraband was a side business that brought in lots of money for him.

He turned at the sound of a bell, the mask falling back into place. He stepped through from the back of his store and greeted his customer, smoothness filling his voice. Tonight he would take steps. He was aware of who the Jester had hired and that person had screwed up. He had a feeling in his gut that he was being watched and that time was running out.

Chapter 7

Leith stood in the back porch after the police had left. He ran his hands through his hair and then scrubbed them down his face. What was going on, he wondered?

He turned as he sensed Regan at the door. He had become more and more aware of her presence around him as the day passed. They had moved past the difficult moments of their first few hours together and the way she had come on the job. She was a good fit for him at work, almost reading his mind. A stray thought crossed his mind that she would be a good fit for him, period. A good fit in his personal life as well.

Regan approached, watching him and then looking down. She had a broom in her hand. Sadness crossed her face at the destruction she saw.

She handed him the broom. "Here. I'll go get the garbage can. Or two. Or three."

"Thanks. Regan." She turned to him as he spoke. "I'm glad you weren't down here when he did this. I wouldn't want you hurt."

She gave him a searching glance, nodded and turned away. He watched her, knowing at some point, he would meddle and poke and prod to find out her history.

Together they worked at cleaning up the mess. Leith stretched. They had been able to salvage a lot of whole tiles. Some of the broken ones they had set aside as possibilities for small areas.

"Do you think you'll have enough?" Regan soft voice sounded from behind him. She was kneeling on the floor, stacking the last few tiles.

"I think so. If not, I'll see if John has more. He did have extras earlier and said he would set them aside for me." Leith carried out the garbage and returned. "Come on, Regan. Let's call it a day. We can finish up tomorrow."

"Okay." Regan's voice was distracted. "Leith, can you get me a flashlight, please? I need some more light."

He handed her his phone with the flashlight icon on. He watched as she reached down into a large crevice between the room floor and the wall. She pulled out a small brown envelope that had worked its way down.

"I don't know what this is, but I don't think it belongs here. It's too new to have been here long." She looked up at him. "We need to get this to Caleb and Ben."

Leith reached out and took the packet. It was slim but he could feel lumps through the paper. "It feels like pebbles or something." He tucked it in his pocket, then held out his hand for Regan.

She stood, deep in thought. "Pebbles." Her eyes flew to Leith. "Do you know where Caleb is right now?"

He shrugged. "I would imagine at home."

"Okay. You lead and I'll follow. This needs to go to him tonight."

Leith stared at her, puzzled. She pushed at him. "Go. Turn off the lights, lock up and let's go."

Caleb held his mug of tea, glad for the warmth on his hands. He was tired. He was tired some days of crime. He was tired of it affecting his family and friends. God was his strength, though, his strong tower. He loved the verses that talked of that. He watched as Hannah moved around the kitchen, cleaning and tidying it up from the meal and readying it for morning. The boys were asleep. He was home early today and had been able to spend time with them.

He reached for Hannah's hand and led her to the living room and together, they sank to the couch. He draped his arm around her and held her close.

Head on his shoulder, Hannah sighed. "I know you, Caleb. What's bugging you?"

He tightened his arm, giving thanks for the wife God had provided. "Nothing here at home. I'm just frustrated at the slowness of finding out what happened, at the block in the investigation."

Hannah went to speak, then stopped as the doorbell rang. It was not usual they had company during the week after supper. Friends knew to give Caleb time with his family.

Caleb sighed, set down his mug of tea, and went to the door. Peeking out, he saw Leith and Regan. He opened the door, greeting them and then indicating the living room. Hannah greeted them and started to rise.

"Please, Hannah, don't leave." Regan asked as she sat beside her.

"What brings you two by?" Caleb glanced between them, picking up on tension.

Leith hesitated, then reached for his pocket. "We were cleaning up and sorting through tiles after you all had left. Regan found this, dropped down in a crevice by the wall." He handed Caleb the packet.

Caleb looked at it, then shot a glance att Leith. Snagging a piece of paper from the office, he laid it on the coffee table. Carefully, he worked to open the sealed envelope. This may be what he had been looking for, the answer to what was going on. Upending it, he shook it slightly.

Hannah and Regan both gasped.

Leith swallowed hard, and then asked, "Is that what I think it is?"

Caleb used his pen to move around the pebbles. He nodded. "They're not pebbles, that's for sure. I will need to send them to the lab, but I suspect they are uncut diamonds. You have may found what the thief was after." He stopped, then continued, "Did you find any other packets?"

Leith shook his head. "That's the only one."

Caleb left, returned with a kraft envelope. He carefully inserted everything in it, sealed it and labeled it. "I'll get this sent off tomorrow. We have an answer in a few days." He caught their eyes with a piercing glance. "I don't need to tell you to be very careful. Smugglers play for keeps."

Regan shivered as she nodded. Why did she feel like the past was catching up with her?

Leith stopped Regan as she was getting in her truck. "I'll follow you home, just to make sure you get there. If you need me, call me."

She nodded. She had hoped that things would be different but it seemed like yesterday all over again. When would it stop?

****

The Jester was not amused. The Innocent had screwed up once again. Those two would not have rushed over here if they hadn't found something. Now the Innocent would need to be dealt with. He wouldn't be able to retrieve that packet, if that's what Caleb had. Caleb was too wary and too smart. The King would be livid. He needed to deal with the issue before he found out and could only hope he didn't lose his own life in the process. The King would consider him dispensable.

Chapter 8

Caleb strode into the station in the morning, eyes searching for Ben. He found him at the coffee station.

"Bring your mug. I have some news." Caleb spoke quietly.

Ben looked, then followed Caleb.

"Shut the door and sit." Caleb dropped into his chair and pulled the envelope from his pocket. "Leith and Regan brought this to me last night. Regan found it when they were cleaning up the mess. It contains what I think are raw diamonds. You were on the money about contraband. I need you to take this Oak City to the lab, but I don't want a big deal made of it. You need a day off, don't you? Take Marg and head into the city. Make a day of it."

Ben nodded. "Sure, that's what they were looking for. Put small packets in the crate, mark the crate and then retrieve them.

Only somehow this time, something got mixed up. I wonder how much we've missed."

Caleb nodded. "That's my fear. I also suspect that it is only going to get worse. I can't put a tail on Regan and Leith. I don't have enough to support that. If I say anything to Liam, he'll smother Leith and that will go over like a lead balloon." He pointed to the packet. "Go. Spend some time with Marg. You've been putting in some long hours." He stopped and watched as his friend tucked away the packet. It wasn't the first time Ben had made a run like that. "Ben." Ben looked up. "I want you to consider something. We have the funding to set up for more training and I would like to see more training in evidence recovery and tracking evidence. I would appreciate it if you could give it some thought. You have the experience and the knowledge. You are also a born teacher. I've seen you work at church. I've seen you work with the young officers here."

Ben stilled. This had been a dream of his. "I'll pray about it and talk it over with Marg."

"Thanks. Not get out of here."

A few hours later, Caleb looked up at a tap at his open door. Liam stood there. He beckoned him in.

Liam shut the door behind him and then sat, staring at him in silence.

Caleb stared back, waiting for Liam to speak.

"Leith called me. Are those really uncut stones?"

Caleb hesitated. "They may be. We need to wait for the lab report."

Liam stood and paced. The anger was palpable. "This is my brother we're talking about. Someone tried to kill him. Are they going to try again?"

Caleb let him speak, knowing he had to vent. "I don't know, Liam. We still need to do a lot of leg work."

Liam looked at him, spun and headed for the door. He stopped, hand on the knob. "Let me know what you find out. I don't want another family member in the same situation Laycee ended up in."

"Liam." Caleb waited but Liam didn't turn. "I will do my best. My department will do their best to keep him and Regan safe. You know that. But you also know that when we are dealing with smugglers and contraband, it is very difficult."

Liam gave a curt nod and then left.

Caleb looked down at the work on his desk and sighed. He had pushed up through the ranks at a rapid pace, always wanting to the chief. When the chief had retired, he has tapped to take over at a young age. Today, he wished someone else had the responsibility. Paperwork had to be done, regardless of what was going one, and so he bent to the task.

****

Joshua and Leith stood together in what would have one time been the front parlour of the house. Looking around, they both looked pleased.

Joshua had a huge smile on his face. "We did it, Leith. We made the deadline early and stayed within budget. God has been good."

Leith smiled and agreed. "That He was. We wouldn't have though if it hadn't been for Regan. She's amazing with the tile work."

Joshua shot his friend a glance atnd nodded. Yes, he thought. Finally someone who interests Leith and shares a passion with him about his work.

Regan stepped in the room and stopped when she saw the two men, hesitating in a nervous manner. Joshua studied her. There was something she was holding back but what?

Leith turned and have her a smile. "Well done, Regan. You have helped us succeed."

Noise at the door drew their attention as Caleb, Hannah, and Liam entered. There would be a quick run-through the house with family and then in about an hour, the homeowners would walk through. Joshua and Leith knew they would be pleased. The house had good bones and had been a pleasure to restore.

"What do you say, shall we gather for dinner at the cafe?" Caleb asked. They agreed and made plans to meet later.

The Innocent stood in front of the Jester, shaking. He knew he had really screwed up this time. He thought he had found all the packets, only to find he had missed one. The King was very angry, he was told. This mistake on his part would cost dearly.

The Jester watched as the fear mounted in the young man. He could smell the fear. This young punk had served his time. It was time to remove the problem. His hand raised, he saw the Innocent's eyes widen. It was too late. A single sound and the Innocent was on the ground, never to rise again.

The Jester swept a look around to make sure he had left nothing to identify him and then turned, walking away from the body and the old abandoned factory. Justice, in his eyes, was done. Now he just had to save his own skin.

****

Leith stood by his truck in the parking lot and waited for Regan to step out of hers. He approached her and stood looking down at her. Her gray eyes met his. She was hesitant again in her manner and he wondered why. He reached for her hand, but she stuck hers in her pocket. Okay, he thought, too soon.

"I usually take a couple of days off after a job is finished and just wander through some towns, taking in the architecture and the sights. Would you like to join me tomorrow on a journey?"

Regan studied him, head tilted to the side. She gave a big sigh and said, "You're not making it easy working for you, you know." At his look, she shook her head. "Never mind."

She headed for the restaurant, Leith on her heels. "You never answered me."

She spun. "Would that trek be in the manner of a date or just two workers out searching for new ideas? It would never work, me dating the boss."

Leith threw his head back and laughed. "Okay, no date. Just two friends out enjoying a day together."

She thought, and then nodded. "All right. What time?"

"I'll pick you up at 8."

Sudden pinging broke through their conversation. Leith leapt for Regan and sweeping her into his arms, dodged behind a truck. He slid to the ground, cradling her and covering her with his body. He knew it wasn't hail and it wasn't a gravel parking lot for stones to be thrown up from tires. That had to be bullets.

The sound of sirens filled the area and red and blue lights reflected from the windows of the parked vehicles and the stores. Officers shoved open their doors and crouched behind them, revolvers at the ready, and searched the area.

There were no more shots. The shooter had accomplished his goal, gathered his evidence and left.

Caleb stepped from the cafe, revolver in hand, and headed for the patrol cars. He quickly sent officers to search the area. Ben approached.

"What happened here?"

Caleb's keen eyes turned on him as he holstered his revolver. "That's what I want to know. We're fortunate there wasn't anyone out here. But what was he shooting at?"

A sudden call caught his attention and he turned. An officer was waving him over towards a truck. Caleb and Ben ran towards him, hearts in mouth. Did they have a victim anyway?

Caleb slid to a halt as he rounded the front of the truck. Leith was on the ground, propped up against a tire, with an unmoving Regan in his arms. Caleb approached slowly and squatted down beside him.

"Leith." He waited. "Leith. Look at me."

Leith's eyes were fixed and staring. Even when Caleb touched his arm, he didn't move. Caleb scanned them both. There was blood on Regan's shoulder but he couldn't tell how bad the wound was, and Leith was not letting her go.

He stood and looked around. Spotting a senior officer, he waved him over and then sent him to the cafe. He would find Liam and bring him out.

"Ben, get the paramedics here. Bring them in on the grass behind the truck."

Ben looked at him. "No sign of the shooter." He sighed. "I guess we aren't done yet, are we?"

"No, my friend. I don't think we are." Caleb stood looking down at Leith. "I want to know which one of these he was after. They've now become targets and we'll need to arrange protection. Talk to Eddie and see what you can arrange. I'm authorizing overtime on this."

Ben nodded, then touched Caleb's arm. Liam stood a vehicle away, a pale and drawn look on his face. Leith and Regan hadn't made it to the cafe, and he had a bad feeling in his gut as Caleb moved towards him, a stern look on his face.

"Caleb..."

"Leith is not hurt, but I can't get his attention. Regan has been wounded. Leith must have taken her down and now I can't get him to release her so I can get her treated. Maybe you can get through to him."

Liam's eyes slid shut. Relief that his brother was okay slid through him, but worry also for the woman who was becoming a real part of their family. "Let me talk to him."

Liam squatted down by his brother, heart in mouth at the look on his face. He didn't remember ever seeing such a look. He placed a hand on Leith's arm.

"Leith." He waited and then spoke his brother's name again. "Let me have Regan. She needs help."

Leith stirred and his arms loosened on Regan. Liam lifted her away from his brother and handed her to Caleb. Quickly the paramedics moved in and took over her care.

"Leith. Come on, buddy, let's get you up." Liam pulled his brother to his feet.

Leith staggered and then caught his balance. The glazed look was fading.

"What happened?" He was finally able to get words out of his throat.

"There was a shooting, Leith. Regan got grazed." Leith's eyes shot past Caleb to the ambulance pulling away. "I need to get your statement but first Liam is going to take you to Emergency to get checked out."

Leith shrugged off their hands. "I'm fine."

"No. You are going and that's that." Liam pulled out the oldest brother card that he seldom had to use. "Caleb. Can you let Laycee know?"

Caleb nodded, and then motioned Eddie over. "Eddie will take you to the hospital. You can't have your vehicles yet until we release the scene."

Leith paced the waiting room at the hospital. He wasn't family and couldn't be with her. It frustrated him. They had tried to find her Uncle John and then her parents, with no success.

Caleb and Ben entered the hospital and headed back into the Emergency Department, stern looks on their faces. Leith exchanged a look with Liam and Laycee. Something was up.

Laycee grasped her brothers' hands and tugged. "Come, sit down. We need to pray. God knows what's happening."

Leith sank on the edge of a chair and half listened to his brother and sister in prayer. His mind was too numb and too muddled to form words, but he knew that God heard even a half-formed whisper. His eyes never left the door behind where he knew Regan was.

He started as an arm slid around him. Laycee had reached out to her brother. He shut his eyes and leaned back. Why did he feel it wasn't over yet?

Chapter 9

Ben came back through the waiting room, phone to his ear, almost on a run. The three Bradleys shared a glance. What was happening?

Caleb came out, hand under Regan's arm. She was pale and unsteady on her feet. He held up a hand to stop them from approaching and turned to Regan. They could see them arguing, Regan shaking her head in an adamant manner. Caleb didn't seem to be giving in though. Bringing Regan with him, he approached.

"Leith and Regan, someone is after one of you," he stated. "Until we can figure out who, we are going to be upping your protection."

Regan jerked her arm back from Caleb's grasp and stomped away. Before they could stop her, she was out the door. Leith moved to follow, but stopped at Caleb's grip. He turned to look at Caleb.

Caleb was shaking his head. "No. You're not going out there. You're a target. I have an officer out there watching for Regan. I figured she'd do this." He looked at Laycee and Liam. "Right now, my main concern is to get these two to safety. Ben was working on a place but got called to another situation. Neither of these two are going home."

Leith was shaking his head. "No, Caleb. I'm not putting anyone else at risk. If whoever it is wants to come after me, let them." He too broke from the group and was gone before anyone could make a move.

Liam headed after his brother on a run. Leith was gone as was Regan. How did they disappear so quickly? Liam heard a noise and looked to his left. He saw Regan and Leith standing with some officers. Good, he thought. Caleb pegged them right.

"They just had to try it, didn't they?" Caleb voice spoke from behind him.

Liam snorted and agreed. "So now what, Caleb? How do we keep them safe? Where to we tuck them? We can't put them out of circulation for months."

Caleb searched his friend's face. "I know. I just wish..." He pulled out his phone and looked. "I need to take this."

Liam walked toward Leith, who refused to meet his eyes. What was he going to do with him?

****

The King turned cold eyes on the Jester, who was sweating profusely even though the air was cold. He didn't speak, just watched in silence as the underling squirmed.

He turned and paced the room and paced back, once more stopping in front of the Jester. A hand reached out and the sound of flesh hitting flesh rang through the room.

"You have cost me a great deal, not just in money," the King stated. "From now on, you are not on your own. You make no decisions except what I tell you. These two gentleman behind you will be with you 24/7 from now on. They will be introduced as your relatives from outside the area, come to visit you."

He paused, stepped away and then came back. "If you step out of line even the tiniest bit, they will deal with you in a manner I doubt you will enjoy. These are my Knights, who defend me and my property. Take care you do not offend."

The Jester could feel the chills running up and down his spine. He had really screwed things up. At a gesture, one of the Knights touched his shoulder and indicated he was to leave. They followed him. They would be his shadow from now on.

The King waited until he heard the outside door close and then in a fit of rage, flung his glass at the wall. It shattered, and liquid slowly flowed down to pool on the floor. If he couldn't get things under control, he was ruined. He needed to find the rest of those packets, and that fool of a Jester had taken away the only real chance he had.

****

Caleb climbed from his vehicle and stared at the house. He shook his head. There just didn't seem to be any way they could catch a break. He breathed a prayer for wisdom and guidance. He certainly had desire to cross that threshold of that home.

Ben came down the steps and stopped beside him, standing in silence, staring across the street. He shook his hand and then looked down at his hands.

Caleb leaned against his cruiser. "What do we have, Ben? Is it John Sullivan?"

Ben nodded. "It is. The paramedics called it when they came. They suspect it was his heart. We're waiting for the coroner."

Caleb's eyes slid shut. Another link in the chain but how did it fit in? "Any chance it's not natural?"

Ben turned his head, then shook it. "I doubt it. John's had bad health for years. He just never said much to anyone. We've been friends since grade school."

Caleb looked up at the house. "Have a team go through it any way. I would rather be sure than have to have them come back." He stopped. "Have you been able to reach Joseph and Rebecca?"

Ben shook his head. "I've tried. I reached their voice mail. Maybe Regan will have a better idea of where they are. They should be home soon. When they left, they were only planning on being gone a month and it's coming up to six weeks. But then, too, they have never taken a vacation." He stopped and swallowed hard. "This is not what they should be coming home to."

Caleb looked up at the sky. The sun was heading down and he had many hours left to get through. He wouldn't be making it home for his boys this night.

He turned, hand on Ben's shoulder. He went to say something and stopped. He tapped his hand a couple of times and then headed back around to the driver's door. "Did you come up with a safe place to stick Leith and Regan?"

Ben shook his head. "Not yet and I highly doubt we'll get them there. I can see Leith grabbing Regan and taking off, hiding them himself. We can't protect him if he does that."

Caleb looked at the house again, hearing John's Border Collie howling. Sage would need to be taken care of. "Bring Sage to Laycee. She'll look after her. Have you found John's son yet?"

Ben once again shook his head. "No. I have no idea where he is." He stopped at a thought and squinted against the sun. "You know, this bit with the break-ins. That fits David's mentality. I can see him doing that very easily."

"You're right. We need to find him. Send out the alert."

****

Caleb slowly walked up to the Evans' door. His heart was breaking for his friends. How was he to tell Regan her uncle was gone?

Regan answered and stepped back. "Caleb, don't even start. I'm not going into protective custody."

Caleb held up his hand. "Let's sit, Regan. That's not why I'm here."

Regan searched his face, seeing the sadness. Her hand came to her mouth and she stumbled. Caleb caught her arm and helped her to sit.

"Not my parents. Please, not my parents."

Caleb looked down, praying for the words. "No, not your parents. It's your uncle. I'm sorry, Regan, he's gone."

Tears welled up as she shook her head. "He can't be. He just can't be." Sobs shook her body.

Caleb stood and walked to the kitchen, returning with a glass of water. He waited until her sobs had softened. "Ben is tracking your parents. Do you have any idea where they might be?"

She shook her head. "No. I talked to them three days ago and they were heading home but they weren't sure what route they were going to take. They were having such a great vacation." She stopped speaking, lost in thought. "Where's David? I just know he had something to do with this."

Caleb tilted his head and studied her. "Why do you say that?"

She snorted. "I know him. I know what he's capable of."

Caleb shook his head. "I don't think so."

Regan stood. "I know my cousin. I know exactly what he is capable of. If you want to find out who is breaking into the store, find him." She stood at the window, arms wrapped around her wait. "I need to be alone, Caleb. Please."

He hesitated, then said, "Call someone to stay with you. I'll let you know when the coroner has released the body. In the absence of anyone else, you'll be the one notified."

When she didn't respond, he left, closing the door softly behind him. He stopped, puzzled at her words. Why would she say that about David?

He turned to look at the door and started back, then hesitated. He would send Hannah and Laycee over in a while. They might be able to help.

Caleb headed back to his office. It would be a long night. He had to determine what needed to be done with Leith and Regan as well as trying to track down her parents.

Ben followed him into his office and shut the door. Caleb sank into his chair with a sign of relief and buried his head in his hands. Days like this were just too much.

He looked up as a cup of tea appeared in line of sight and nodded his thanks. Somehow, he was going to have to find time for some food.

Ben sat in silence, nursing his own cup of coffee. He shook his head at his thoughts.

"Any luck, Ben?"

Ben nodded. "I managed to find Joseph and Rebecca. They're about six hours away. Joseph said they had planned to stop for the night but would grab a bite to eat and keep driving. They were worried about Regan. Did you ever find David?"

Caleb shook his head. "I was going to ask you that." He leant back in his chair and steepled his fingers. "Regan said something strange tonight before I left her. She asked if I have found David. She is convinced he had something to do with the break-ins."

Ben studied his hands. Caleb waited him out, knowing he liked to put his thoughts in order before speaking.

Ben spoke. "I haven't said much as I haven't proven it totally yet, but David's fingerprints were in the Bell House and also on a some of the imported tile crates. John said he hadn't worked for him for months and that these crates had come in after David had left. He felt bad saying anything but he was too honest not to."

Caleb ran his hand through his hair. "Well, I guess we won't be able to ask John anything more on that. I wonder if he said anything to Joseph. We'll have to wait on that one. It makes one wonder how well Regan got on with David."

Ben looked at him with a seriousness Caleb seldom saw. "You're about the same age as David. Regan is I think about four years younger. You wouldn't have seen much, being young yourself. David always has had a vicious, mean streak to him. John worried about him. My feeling has always been that Regan took a lot of the brunt of it from David. David was adopted as a young child and never felt he fit in. John did tell me he had had to write him out of ownership of the store; David knew this and handled it very poorly."

"That certainly puts a different light on things, now doesn't it."

A tap came at the door and when asked, Annie entered. She handed Ben some papers and left.

Ben studied them and then handed them to Caleb. Caleb looked and then his eyes shot to Ben. "Five hundred thousand dollars in uncut stones just in that packet. The report says they are almost perfect."

"Five hundred thousand reasons to kill. This just changes the whole game we've been playing."

"That it does. Now we have to figure out if they are meant for someone here or if this was just a drop off site on the way through."

Ben leaned back and looked at the ceiling, his lips moving silently in prayer. He dropped his head back. Caleb was watching him.

"Go home, Ben. Get some sleep. You'll think better then."

Ben nodded and stood. "Follow your own advice, Caleb. This is far from over. You'll need more strength that you know before it is."

Neither knew how prophetic those words would be.

Chapter 10

Five days later, the funeral for John Sullivan was over and the will had been read. Regan and her father were now sole owners of the business. There had been no word on David. He had not shown up anywhere.

Regan slowed as she approached the house where she knew she would find Leith. She was torn. Her father had been adamant that he would not need her in the store. He wanted her to follow her dream and if that dream was setting tile, then that was what he was pushing her to do. She needed to talk to Leith. He had been there in the background over the last few days, comforting in his presence but they had not had time to talk.

She shut her truck door and drew in a deep breath. She had no idea how this was going to go. She stepped into the house. It was not a big job, not a renovation like the last one, but there was enough tile work to keep both of them busy. She headed for the kitchen, where she could hear his clear whistle. Stopping in the doorway, she watched him.

Sensing her presence, Leith stopped and then turned. His gaze went to the clear gray eyes he was beginning to learn to love. He said not a word.

Regan stepped forward and stopped, rubbing her hand on the countertop and studying the backsplash he was working on. It was simple, just a few colours, but striking in how he had planned the layout.

She didn't look at him. "Well, Leith, where do we go from here?"

He waited for her to look up and when she didn't ducked his head. "Nothing has changed. If you still want to work for me, then you should. If you want to go work with your Dad, then do that."

She sighed. "I didn't think it would be so hard to make a decision."

"Mom would always ask if we had prayed about our decisions. Don't rush to make one. Spend the time in prayer. Remember that you are not alone in your decisions. Whenever you feel frightened about what you are deciding, run to that strong tower God has provided."

She tilted her head. "How do you always know exactly what to say to me?" She turned. "My kit is in the truck. Where do I start?"

Leith laughed. This was his Regan, back on track.

As they sat at lunch, Leith asked about John's dog.

"I have her. Sage is such a sweetheart but she is grieving. People don't expect dogs to grieve but they do. It will take some time but I'll do my best with her."

****

The ragged clothing on the man denoted his status in society, a lowly of the low. He stumbled through a haze into the abandoned building, looking for shelter. He stopped. What was that stench?

He turned and almost ran from the building. Stumbling through the debris on the building's parking lot, he exited to the street. Coming towards him was a patrol car. He waved at it and then stumbled as he lost his balance.

Eddie opened his door and approached the vagrant. Hearing his words, his eyes shot to the building and then back to the man. Keying up his mike he asked for assistance.

Caleb pulled to a stop behind a cruiser and got out. He was never ready to hear of a body being found. Ben approached him.

"Any identification yet?"

Ben shook his head. "Not that I know of. Eddie's around here somewhere. He's the one old Charlie flagged down."

Caleb took a look around. "Where's Charlie?"

"Eddie sent one of the officers with him to the diner up the street. He thought if he could get some food into him, he might be more alert and answer questions."

Caleb and Ben looked around as footsteps approached them.

"What do you have, Eddie? Any I.D.?"

Eddie shook his head. "It looks as if the body was stripped of anything of value, either before he was killed or after. The coroner thinks six to seven days but he'll know more after the autopsy. This is the only thing he found " Eddie held up a clear evidence bag with a key on a key ring.

Caleb reached for it, then tilted it towards Ben. "Sullivan's."

Eddie nodded, then looked back at the decrepit building. "The body has similarities to John's son. I have a suspicion that's him and that's why we couldn't find him for the funeral."

Caleb stilled. David Sullivan. What was his tie to everything? They already suspected him for the break-ins but what was he looking for? Was it the packets of jewels like they had found?

"Tell the coroner to call me once he's done the preliminary." Caleb motioned for Ben to follow him.

Ben spoke. "What was it we were saying a couple of days ago? If this is David, there could go our link to the gang."

"I don't think we're done. They will want that packet Regan found. I suspect there are still packets in crates at the store.

I'll talk to Joseph about having a search done for the shipments from outside the country that we were tracking. Did you ever determine if the packets were inserted on the route or not?"

Ben shook his head. "Can't. Not enough information. Until we crack this, we won't know."

"That's it then. Okay, carry on. Did you get the arrangements made for more patrols and cover for Leith and Regan?"

"Since I can't get them to cooperate, all I can do is send more patrols around their homes and if men are available and willing for overtime, have a car sit outside. It's not the best solution but it's what we have for now."

Caleb nodded, knowing Ben had tried. Things seemed to have settled down, but his gut said otherwise and he had learned to go with his gut feeling.

****

Ben stepped into Caleb's office and shut the door, sitting down while he waited for the phone conversation to end. He studied the report in his hand, not liking what he had to tell Caleb.

Caleb's call ended and he stared at Ben, who silently handed the folder to him. Caleb opened and read through the report quickly, then read back through more slowly. He dropped the folder on his desk and buried his head in his hands. Now what?

"It's David Sullivan." At Ben's nod, he drew a deep breath. "Get us a search warrant for John's house and David's place. I'll talk to Joseph and see if David had anything at the store. We may need a search warrant for there."

Ben spoke up. "I don't understand. John loved that boy so much."

Caleb's gaze searched for answers across the room and found none. "I know. Good parents can have bad kids. Once you have the warrants, get started on the search. Keep it to as few as possible. There's still something going on in this town, I can feel it. Somehow, it almost feels as if there's leak somewhere and I would trust all our people with my life."

"I know that feeling, Caleb. Just keep praying. We'll get it sorted out."

Later that afternoon, Caleb parked outside Joseph and Rebecca's home. He didn't want to make this call, didn't want to make this notification. It was too soon after John.

Rebecca answered the door and after greeting him, invited him back to the kitchen. She put a cup of tea in front of him and went to find Joseph.

Caleb stood and shook Joseph's hand before they were all seated once again.

"I am really sorry about John."

"Thank you, Caleb. He never did tell us how sick he was. I guess that's why he pushed Rebecca and I to go on that trip. But that's not why you're here. It is about Regan?" Joseph's keen eyes searched Caleb's face.

Caleb stared at his tea and then raised his eyes, shaking his head. "No, not that I'm aware of. We're still investigating what's going on with the store. It's David."

He saw Rebecca hand fly to her mouth and Joseph reach for her other hand.

"We found his body early this morning in an abandoned factory on the east side of town. I'm sorry to have to be the one to tell you this."

Joseph's face hardened and tears flowed down Rebecca's face. "What happened?"

Caleb drew in a breath. What he had to say now was the hard part and would be devastating to the family. "It wasn't an accident. David was shot once. The coroner figures it was at least a week ago."

"Before John died." Rebecca whispered and Caleb nodded.

"We have search warrants for David's place and also for John's. It's standard procedure. I know you can give permission for John's but we'll do it by the book."

After speaking with them for a while and calling for their pastor and his wife to come over, Caleb stepped outside. Joseph followed him out.

"What aren't you saying in front of Rebecca?"

Caleb stared at the night sky, amazed at the clarity of it and the number of stars he could see. He needed to remember that God was in control, the Creator of the stars was also the Creator of man, and the Author of a man's life.

"We may need to search the store. It is looking more and more like David was involved in the break-in at the store and the incident at the Bell House."

Joseph too looked at the sky. "What you're saying doesn't surprise me. He was an unhappy child and an even more unhappy man. John and his wife did their best but could never really reach to his heart. He got involved with a rough crowd early in high school. Things would happen. He always denied his involvement." He stopped, then continued, "Talk to Regan. She never liked him, never wanted to even be in the same room as he was. She has never said but I think he had something to do with her moving away for those 10 years. If that's the case, that young man cost us precious time with our daughter." He stopped, laid a hand on Caleb's shoulder, and then headed back into the house to his wife. They had another funeral to plan.

Chapter 11

Ben met Caleb as he stepped from his car in front of the rundown shack David called home. "You wouldn't think a son of John's would live is such squalor, would you?"

Caleb shook his head. "I don't think John was able to do anything. Joseph mentioned last night that John didn't seem to have any influence on his son at all. What did you find?"

"The team is just getting started but it looks as if he was into some pretty heavy stealing and has been for some time. It will explain some of the thefts from around town. They'll be looking hard to find out if he has any information on that packet Regan found."

Caleb thought for a minute. "I'm sure you're right. Joseph has given permission for us to search John's house, even though we have a warrant, and also the store. He wants answers." Caleb stopped. "He said something interesting though." Caleb stopped for a minute, watching traffic move by. "He followed me out of the house and we were talking about Regan. He told me Regan had no use for her cousin, wouldn't be around him. He always felt that David had something to do with her leaving town."

Ben thought about that for a few minutes. His keen eyes watched the activity around the shack. "I could see that. Regan has that ability to read people. She has an intuition not many people have. I would trust her instincts any day."

Caleb turned to look at Ben. "Really?"

Ben nodded. "I've known her all her life. Joseph and Rebecca are good friends. She would say something about a person, even as a child, and almost 100% of the time, she would be right on with her comments."

"We need to talk to her and soon."

Eddie approached them with a clear evidence bag in his hand, handing it silently to Caleb. Caleb studied it, then shot a look at Eddie. "Any more like this?"

Eddie shook his head. "We're still looking but this definitely ties him to the incident at the Bell House."

Caleb handed the bag to Ben. In it, the evidence team had placed paper from a tile crate, clearly marked. The mark didn't have anything to do with the type of tile or the manufacturer.

"This is good. Now we know what we are looking for." Ben handed the bag back to Eddie. "Make sure this information doesn't get out. I will personally fire anyone who leaks even a tidbit of news about this."

"I'll make sure."

Ben and Caleb looked at each other. Their thoughts were similar. Now they were making progress.

Three days later, Regan wandered around her parents' home. She really needed to find her own place. Her uncle's dog, Sage, kept pace with her. Regan reached down and patted the silky coat.

The threat from David was gone. She should have spoken up years ago, but God had known where He wanted her. She would be back at work tomorrow, and immersing herself in the pattern and colours of the tiles would help. She loved that part of the work, taking the rough paper pattern and translating it into finished work. She thought, that is just what God does—He takes the roughness of our lives and translates them into His workmanship, His creation.

Leith approached her, watching intently as she stopped. "We need a break, Regan. We need to get away, just like we had planned."

Regan shook her head. "No, I want to work."

Leith stopped her with a hand on her arm. When she wouldn't look at him, he commanded, "Look at me, Regan." Her eyes flew to his. "You need a chance to get away from here, a chance to do something that takes your mind off what has happened."

Regan looked at him and gave a small smile. "Looking out for me again, are you?"

Leith's hand came up and he gently touched her cheek. "I'll pick you up tomorrow morning at 8 and we'll do the town.   Wear something casual and comfy shoes." He hesitated. "Thank you, Regan, for doing this."

Regan watched him walk away, her fingers on her cheek where he had touched it.   No, she thought, thank you, Leith Bradley. Thank you for caring.   You are making me care too much and I just can't do that again.

****

The King turned from his store front window and paced the store. Business was really down and he had no idea why. People weren't buying.   He really needed those packets. Now he would never find them, thanks to that fool of a Jester.

He would need to deal with him shortly. But first, he needed his Knights to find those two who had interfered and bring them to him. He would deal with them and then the Jester.

After that he would pack up and move, retiring from his store, go overseas to some warm climate.

He motioned forward his one Knight and gave his orders. They would be carried out in a summary manner.

****

Liam watched his brother and sister as they played with Laycee's Sheltie. Defiant certainly seemed to be winning the battle for the ball. He loved this dog. He looked down as he felt something hit his leg and picked up Laycee's tuxedo cat, Terror. She cuddled down in his arms, licked his hand, then sat staring around with her intense green eyes. He still didn't know what to make of a cat that sang and chirped her way through the day.

Laycee came back into the house, shutting the door behind him. Leith had sat on the deck steps and Defiant had crawled into his knee. "We need to get him a dog."

Liam laughed. "Yes, I think we do. Why do I think you have one in mind?"

Laycee smirked. "That's because I do. I know of a trainer whose dog has had puppies. One would be perfect for Leith. Or even for you."

Liam held up his hand. "I don't think so. I'm not a dog person."

"No? Then why is Defiant, my stand-off Sheltie, all over you when he sees you? And for that matter, why is Terror is your arms? You're not a 'cat person' either, you say."

Liam shrugged. "What can I say? It's my magnetic personality."

Laycee swatted her brother. "Please." She turned and looked back at Leith. "He's got it bad, doesn't he?"

Liam broke out in laughter, startling Terror who sprang from his arms and raced through the house. "And you don't?" He hugged his sister. "I am so glad for you. I hated what you went through, but God brought you the mate you needed."

Laycee tilted her head back. "Yes, He did. Joshua is that." She gave him a saucy look. "Now, we need to work on you."

Liam shook his head as she headed for the front of the house. Laycee was Laycee and loved by many.

Leith stepped back into the house, shutting the door as Defiant's plushy tail cleared it. "I'm off. I'll let you stay and hear the wedding talk. I'm glad Laycee's settled."

"Me too, brother." Liam stopped speaking, watching his brother. Leith was tired and worn and it showed in his face. His face was drawn and there were lines that hadn't been there just a few weeks ago. "How are you doing?"

Leith shrugged, not meeting his brother's eyes. Liam moved towards his brother, hands coming up to grip his shoulders.

Leith looked up. "I'm getting there. It's been a tough few weeks."

Liam drew his brother into a bear hug and then released him. "Take some time. You need it."

Leith smirked. "That's what I'm doing tomorrow, taking some time," he shot over his shoulder as he headed for the door and his truck.

Liam shouted with laughter. "And I suppose taking time tomorrow won't include someone by the name of Regan?"

"I'm not telling." He shut the door on Liam's renewed laughter.

"What's he not telling?" Laycee stuck her head back into the kitchen.

"He's off tomorrow with Regan, probably to do one of those wander through a small town days he loves."

Laycee's eyes shone. "Wonderful. Now come, I need you to look at something."

"Not wedding stuff!" Liam groaned.

"Stop it. You're having a ball with this and you know it."

Liam's arm draped over his sister's shoulder. She was so right. He was having a ball and enjoying every moment of her romance she cared to share with him.

Chapter 12

Leith helped Regan into his truck and then moved around to climb behind the wheel. She had taken him at his word and dressed in coloured jeans, a soft green sweater that highlighted her hair so well, and denim jacket. Comfortable leather shoes finished it all off.

"So where are we off to?"

Leith pulled away. Today was going to be wonderful, he thought. "When I take a day off, I like to wander through small towns, just to see what life is like somewhere else. I often get ideas for designs in some of the older homes that are open to the public."

"That's sounds like a fun day. Which town?"

"I thought Elmtown. I haven't been there in a couple of years."

"I haven't been there for many years. It sounds fun."

Conversation drifted through many topics. Leith kept checking his rearview mirror.

"Are we being followed?" Regan's voice broke through his thoughts.

"I'm not sure. I've had the feeling I've been followed for days, but the vehicles seem to change. I thought maybe it was Caleb's doing, but this vehicle is not obvious like an officer would be."

Regan shot a glance out the back window, then at him. "Today, we're not worrying about that. You promised your 'friend' a day away from work. Now, let's get at it." She laughed.

Leith laughed as well. "You've got it."

Still uncomfortable at the thought of being followed, Leith watched the traffic behind him. He was looking forward to this day and didn't want anything to ruin it.

Leith and Regan spent the day wandering in and out of shops, small stores, and homes open to the public. Regan could see why Leith said he got a lot of ideas. A shared lunch of fresh-cut fries and fresh cider halted their adventure in the middle of the day, although Regan laughingly protested it wasn't a healthy meal. Leith shrugged, told her she was on vacation, and to eat up.

Late in the day, they made their way to the little foot bridge that crossed a small brook in a nearby park. Leith reached for Regan's hand and held on tight when she tugged at it. She finally relaxed and then he felt her hand grip his. She stopped in the middle of the bridge, recovered her hand, and leaned forward to look down.

"This is so peaceful. I could stay here for a long time."

"I could too." Leith agreed, watching her face. He had seen it relaxing over the day. "I'm glad you agreed to come."

She laughed. "Yes, friend. I'm glad too. We needed this." She looked into the distance. "I'm glad." She repeated herself, then turned to look at him.

Leith stood, hip resting again the railing, and facing her. His eyes traced her face.

"Leith," she spoke hesitantly. "I really need to talk to someone. I think you're it."

"About what?" His voice was calm but his heart was racing. Here is comes, he thought, she's about to say she has met someone else.

"About David." She stopped as her eyes flew past him. A figure dressed in black and with a ski mask covering the face was approaching them. "Leith. Behind you."

Leith spun, hands in the air ready to defend them, He heard Regan give a cry behind him and shot a glance over his shoulder. A second figure, clad like the first, stood behind her, arm around her neck and revolver to her head. His eyes danced between the two men. There was no way he could get her away without one of them getting hurt. He kept his hands up but opened the fists in a sign of surrender.

The men shoved them off the bridge away from town. Pushing them through the undergrowth, they came to a black van. The door was opened and they were shoved in. Cloth was tied over their eyes and their hands were roughly brought behind their back and tied.

Regan shifted over as close to Leith as she could get. Her thoughts flew, her mind raced. Who and what? She lifted up prayer after prayer as she tried to keep her balance on the floor of the van.

Leith surged with anger. How did he let this happen? Who were these men? What did they want? He felt Regan close to him and so desperately wanted to hug her to reassure her. He struggled with his bonds but the men were professionals. The bonds were not loosening.

After numerous twists and turns and who knew how long, the vehicle stopped. He could feel the shift in it as the men stepped out. There was a low conversation, then the door of the van opened. Leith was pulled out and he heard a cry from Regan as she was roughly dragged out. He was helpless and he hated that feeling.

They were pushed into a building, he could tell by the change of temperature and light. It smelled old, as if it hadn't been used in years. Up a long flight of stairs they were made to walk and down a hallway.

Rasping sounds came as a lock was opened and then the grating of rusty rings as a door was pulled open. They were shoved inside. Leith stumbled, caught his balance and turned.

"What do you want?" he demanded.

"You'll find out. The King will be asking the questions in the future, not you."

Leith's head turned from side to side as he tried to track the voices and the footsteps. He heard a small cry from Regan, then felt a prick on his shoulder. His body grew faint and he collapsed. He couldn't protect her. Lord, save her, he cried as the darkness won.

****

Caleb set his mug of tea on his kitchen counter and caught up his phone. It was Liam. As he listened, his face paled and his heart sank.

"I'm on my way, Liam. Sit tight."

Caleb approached Liam standing on Leith's porch. "Have you been inside?"

"No. I noticed the door was open a bit, pushed it open and called for Leith. He hasn't answered."

"Stay here. I have officers on the way. I'm going in."

Caleb drew his revolver and entered, searching each room as he made his way through the house. Leith was not there, but whoever had been had done a good job on searching. It was a mess.

Caleb came back out and stopped by Liam. "He's not in there that I can see. It's been tossed so someone was looking pretty hard for something. Let the team work through it."

Liam stared back through the door at the damage he could see. He shook his head. "What is happening in our town, Caleb? And why us?"

Caleb watched as the evidence team and responding officers approached and drew Liam off to the side. "I don't know, Liam. I really don't know." He drew him to the side. "Track down Leith and see if you can find him."

Liam glared at Caleb. "I'll try but I have a bad feeling about this." He turned and stormed away.

Caleb watched, then shook his head. He had to agree. Something was going on in their town.

Later, Caleb approached the Evans' home. There was no one home. He then tried the store. Both Regan's parents were adamant she had not come home last night. They knew she had planned to be away the day before but Regan hadn't said with whom. Caleb had a pretty good idea it was Leith but it was not like either one of them not to come home or call if they had had any trouble with a vehicle. Something stank.

****

Leith stirred, his body moving restlessly on the dirty, garbage-strewn floor. His mouth felt so dry and bitter-tasting. He rolled to his side and tried hard to open his eyes. They cracked a bit and then fell shut once again. He was just too tired to try again.

Hours later, he felt hands on his arm and shoulder and a gentle shaking. A soft hand touched his face. "Leith." He knew that voice. Whose was it?

Regan shook Leith again. She just had to get him awake. They needed to get away while they could.

Leith rolled to his back and groaned. Eyes opening, he stared up and then focused on Regan. Her worried face was bent over his.

"Leith, we need to move. We need to get going." She tried to raise him up but he was too heavy and his body wasn't cooperating.

He tried to wet dry lips and croaked, "Give me a minute." He gathered his strength and managed to get upright, head spinning as he did. Her arm came around him to support him.

"How long?"

"I don't know. It's daylight so I think it's the next day." Regan's eyes shot around the room. "We need to get out of here. I don't see any way but the door and it's locked tight. The only windows are those tiny ones up at the top."

Vision clearing, Leith scanned the area. She was right. They didn't have many options. They couldn't even surprise someone coming in—the door opened to the hallway.

"Help me up. I'll see what I can find." Leith staggered to his feet and swayed as he regained his balance.

Gaining strength and balance, Leith felt his way along the walls and then again. He stopped by the door. Yes, he had felt a weak spot.

Beckoning Regan over, he whispered, "See if you can find a piece of metal bar or wood that I can use. It's weak here."

Regan frantically searched the large room, finally finding a piece of metal pipe under the debris. She rushed with it over to Leith. He looked at her and grinned, then surprised her with a quick kiss. He winked and then moved to work on the weakened metal.

Regan's fingers went to her mouth. Leith's actions had surprised her. But it was a good surprise. When they got out of here, she would ask him what he meant by that.

Leith worked as quickly and as quietly as he could. The metal gave bit by bit. Soon, he was able to shove it back enough for Regan to step through. A little more, and he was free. He caught her hand in his and moved towards the stairs, listening as he went. He looked over the railing and leaned over just enough to see. No one seemed to be there. He pulled Regan after him down the stairs. Hesitating for a moment, he headed to the back of the building. Whatever it had been, the equipment had been removed. There were scattered crates and metal but nothing big enough for them to hide behind if they had to. They reached the back door and he shoved. It creaked. He stopped, heart in mouth. If anyone was here, they would have heard it. He shoved again and they were out. There was an area they had to cross that was open but he figured if they were quick, they would be through it and into the woods on the other side before they were seen.

Clasping Regan's hand tighter, he pointed to the woods, and waited until she nodded. Another glance around and the race was on. They had made it. Now he just had to figure out where they were and how to get back home, all the while keeping Regan safe.

They walked as carefully as they could, trying their best not to leave a trail or make a noise. It was hard. The woods had really become overgrown at this point. Finally, Regan tugged on his hand.

"I need to stop, Leith. I need to rest. I can't go on."

He turned. She was right. They did need to rest. "I can hear water over there. If it's clear, we can get some and rest a bit too."

****

The Jester looked around the room where they had hidden Leith and Regan. They were gone, vanished into thin air. He looked at the wall by the door and the opening Leith had created and then down at the metal pipe on the floor. How had they missed that? The two Knights had searched the room.

The King would have his head. His head would roll. The Knights knew they were in trouble too. He could tell by the way they were moving. The blame would fall on him though. He was the one who had found this place and assured the King that those two couldn't get out. How was he ever going to explain this?

He turned, not seeing the hand raised towards him. A single shot and he fell. The Jester's life had come to an inglorious end. No one would ever find him here.

The two Knights looked at one another and then left. They needed to find those two. Searching the grounds, they found no sign of where they had gotten to. Whispered conversation and they turned to stare at the woods. That had to be where they were but how would they find them there? Neither of them wanted to be the one to tell the King the situation as it now stood. They had agreed they needed a search dog and they knew just where to find one. Leith's home town was known for its search and rescue team. One of those dogs would do. The owner wasn't needed.

****

"Leith, I need to stop. I need to rest." Regan gasped.

He looked around. "I can hear water. Over there." He pulled her with him until they reached a small stream. "Wait."

144

When he was certain, it was okay he led them forward. Regan dropped gratefully to her knees and greedily sucked up water. Leith stopped her.

"Careful. Not too much at once."

He sat back on his heels and scanned the area, hazel eyes searching. "We need to keep moving, but I have no idea where we are."

Regan shook her head as well. "I have no idea either. The way they kept moving, it confused me. Not being able to see didn't help."

"Take another drink. We need to get moving."

They slowed their pace and continued moving away from the stream and the building. Dusk was falling.

"Leith, we need to stop. We can't go on in the dark."

He nodded. "I know. Let's see where we can hole up for the night."

Chapter 13

The King stared at his Knights. His rage was palpable.

"What do you mean they have escaped? I thought you had them where they were unable to get out. You're all a bunch of fools." Spittle flew from his mouth as he continued to berate them. He stopped.

"That one. Get rid of him."

The Knights looked at each other and one spoke. "The Jester has been taken care of. We have a plan to find them."

After they left, the King stormed around his office. It was all falling apart. When would it end?

****

Caleb looked up at the commotion at the front of the station and then moved forward. He could see Anna Welch talking with the officer working the front desk. When she saw him, she motioned for him.

"What's up, Anna?"

"It's Betsy, my search and rescue dog. Someone has stolen her from her kennel. I was out for about an hour and came home and she's gone."

"Give us the details and we'll canvas your neighbourhood. No chance of the kennel getting open on its own?"

She shook her head. "I have a lock on it when I'm out. The lock was cut."

Caleb rubbed his neck. Who would want a search and rescue dog? He spun.

"Anna, I think I know why. I can't say right now."

Caleb headed back for his office and motioned Ben in.

"I think Anna's dog, Betsy, was taken to try and find Leith and Regan. They're starting to get desperate."

"No word from them yet?"

Caleb shook his head. "Both the Bradleys and the Evans said they would call if they had heard anything and they haven't.

Where are they? Without a clue, we have no idea where to search for them." He looked up at a knock at his door.

Eddie stood there. "Caleb, I just got word Leith's truck has been found in Elmtown. I'm headed over there to speak with the responding officer."

Caleb nodded. "Let them know what's happening here and see if they had any word."

Caleb drew a deep breath. Things were happening, he had no idea what, and he had no idea who or how to respond.

"I'll give Liam a call. He'll want to head that way."

Caleb agreed. "It's not our town but it's just over the area we patrol. Let's hope wherever they are, they are headed this way."

****

The sun rose on a new day. Leith stirred quietly, not wanting to disturb Regan, but he knew they had to get moving. He gently awakened her and they moved off. He hoped he was headed in the right direction.

A noise made his stop.   Regan screamed and then her scream was cut off. A black figure stood in front of him.   A sudden blow to the abdomen doubled him over and he dropped to his knees, blackness blocking out the slight and sending him gasping for air.

Regan struggled to free herself but the grip was strong.   She finally braced her hands on the arm around her waist, stretched herself as far forward as she could.   She could feel the breath on the back of her head.   She slammed her head backwards and heard bones crunch.   She was released and stumbled forward.   That was not a good idea.   Her head was hurting now.   She grabbed a nearby branch and lunged at the man standing over Leith.   Before he could turn, she brought it down over his head. With a groan, the man collapsed.

Regan hurried to Leith's side and dropped to her knees.   Lifting his face, she said, "We need to go."

Turning from him she grabbed up the knapsacks and guns the men had dropped. She saw a dog standing nearby and went towards it.   She knew the dog.   It was Betsy, a friend's dog. She caught the leash and came back to Leith. Helping him to his feet, she tucked a shoulder under his arm. They disappeared from sight.

The two Knights staggered to their feet and looked around. They reached for the packs and guns and found them gone. They had other weapons on them. They searched and found the trail. This time, they would not fail. They would find those two and bring them to the King.

Leith stopped. "I need a breather."

Regan looked worriedly behind her. "We can't stop long. They'll be coming."

"I know. Just for a moment, then we'll get moving."

Noise from in front of them stopped them. Sudden blows rained down on them to the barking of the dog and they sank into blackness. They had not made it out.

****

"Caleb." He turned at the voice behind him. "How you found them yet?"

He shook his head. "Not yet, Liam. They were seen around town two days ago but it looks as if they never made it back to his truck. There are just so many places they could be."

Liam's face was drawn. Where was his brother? He looked at his brother's truck and closed his eyes in prayer.

"So what do we know?"

Caleb motioned and led him over to a nearby picnic table.

"We do know that David Sullivan was involved in the break-ins; we have proof. We found his body a few days ago. We also have that packet Leith and Regan found. It contained uncut jewels. We are trying to track the source of them. Somewhere along the delivery route the packets of jewels are being inserted into the crates of tiles. We have some ideas as to who is to receive them but aren't releasing any more information yet."

Liam buried his head in his hands. He was at the point where he felt so helpless. With Laycee, he was able to help. Now, he just didn't know what to do.

"So, where do we go from here?"

Caleb looked at his notes. He was at a loss too. He didn't think they would find anything in or on the truck. It looked like Leith had locked it and walked away.

Ben approached and motioned for him to come.

"I'll be right back, Liam." He stopped, laid his hand on his friend's shoulder. "You're carrying those burdens again, my friend. You know where to lay them."

Ben spoke, "I have someone who saw Leith and Regan taken away."

Caleb's glance shot to Ben's. "Where and when?"

"There's a little park over the way. The witness says he saw them standing on the bridge, then a dark-clothed figure approached from either side. They forced Leith and Regan to go with them."

"Did the witness get a good look?"

Ben shook his head. "It's a younger fellow, in his early teens, but very good at detail. He said they were in black and seemed to have paint on their faces, like they were playing war."

Caleb stilled. "Camouflage paint." He sighed. "Not a lot to go on."

Ben stood and looked into the distance. "I don't like this. This is too organized. Whoever is behind it has big bucks to spend."

"I know. I wonder." Caleb looked back at Liam, then back to Ben. "I have an idea and I need to you run some background information. Dig as deep as you have to." He scrawled a name on a page from his notebook, ripped it out, and handed it to Ben.

Ben took a look at the name and his eyebrows raised. Then, he nodded. "That does make sense. Too much sense. Let me see what I can find out. I have some contacts at the federal level that can help."

Caleb walked back to Liam. "We'll have Leith's truck towed back to our yard and go over it. I doubt we'll find much though."

Liam looked up. "What aren't you telling me?"

Caleb sank down on the bench on the other side of the table. His face was troubled. He glanced at the sky, trying to gather his thoughts and words. "We have an eye witness who saw Leith and Regan

153

abducted the day they were here and forced into the woods. The department here will set up a search, but I think they're back into our area somewhere."

Liam's breath caught in his throat and his eyes slid shut. Please Lord, not that.

Caleb's hand settled on his arm. "We don't know the details. Keep the faith, my friend. God is in control. Leith will figure out a way to get them out of there."

Liam couldn't answer. First Laycee, now Leith. What was happening to his family? All of a sudden, he didn't feel like the brother who should be able to protect them. He felt like a scared little boy who wanted his parents.

Caleb watched the emotions flickering across his friend's face. He sent up prayers for him, for Laycee, for the department to find answers, but even more that Leith and Regan would be kept safe, wherever they were.

It was late and Caleb was back in his own office. Eddie stuck his head in the door.

"We have another body."

Caleb closed his eyes. Please Lord, just please not one of them.

"It's Eric Brand. He was a friend of David Sullivan."

Caleb sat back. "Eric Brand. Now that's a name that has meant trouble in this town. Run with it, Eddie. Let me know what you find."

"Will do."

Caleb looked at the paperwork on his desk and then locked it away. Tomorrow would do. He needed time with his wife and family.

Liam stood behind Laycee, hands on her shoulders. Tears were running down her face and neither Liam or Joshua had been able to help her.

"Caleb's trying, Laycee. He's really trying."

"I know. I just wish they were here. Why didn't we know they weren't back that night?"

"I don't know. Leith has been pretty good about that but he is entitled to his privacy. We don't talk every day, so it wasn't unusual for us not to hear from him."

She nodded, then turned to hug her brother. He wrapped his arms and held on tight. Tears were in his eyes too.

"I want my Mom and Dad," she whispered.

Tears did fall then from Liam's eyes, dropping onto her black hair. "I know, honey. I know. So do I. I miss their prayers."

Joshua stood watching the siblings, devastation in his face. Now he understood how Liam and Leith and Caleb had felt last year when he and Laycee were missing.

Liam released his sister and turned her to Joshua. "Take care of her, Joshua." Unable to articulate another word, he turned and almost ran from her home.

Looking at the sky, his anger burned. How could he find his brother? Then he sobered.

"God, you're in control. Protect them. Bring them home."

Chapter 14

Leith stirred, moving restlessly. His abdomen hurt and so did his head. He couldn't remember why. Eyes cracking open, he blinked and then gazed around. Where was he? The room was smaller. There were windows but he couldn't tell if it was night or day. His eyes ran around the room. There was a sectioned-off area in the back. The door looked solid from what he could see. He continued to move his eyes, then the world spun and he dropped back into darkness.

Regan sat beside Leith, watching him. He had been awake and had slipped back into unconsciousness. She felt defeated. Where are you, God? Why didn't You prevent this? Why didn't you let us get away? She reached out and laid her hand on Leith's head. She needed him to wake up. She had no idea how long they had been there or who had taken them. The last thing she remembered was that they were running from those men.

Betsy! She rose to her knees and searched. Betsy wasn't there. Oh, Betsy, please make your way home. Please find us again.

Sounds came at the door and she moved to lay silently where she had awakened. She stilled her breath as much as she could to mimic the unconscious state she had been left in. Her head hurt so she knew she had been hit at some point.

Eyes closed, she heard the lock open and then the door. Boot steps crossed the room, stopping first by Leith and then another set crossed to her. She kept still. Please don't let them touch me, she prayed. A boot toe prodded her. She kept the groan inside. The boots waited and then walked away. She cracked her eyes just a bit and watched. The men stood for a few moments watching them and then walked away.

"How hard did you hit them?" The voice said.

"Not that hard. They shouldn't still be out. I have no idea what the King is going to say. You know how he handles problems."

She knew at least one of those voices. Her memory was fogged but eventually she would remember. Darkness closed in on her again and she slept.

****

Hannah watched her husband in their yard. He was wandering, mug of tea in hand. She listened—the boys were still sleeping. She opened the door and crossed to where he had stopped, staring at the waterfall that would soon be flowing again.

Her arm around him, she leaned on him. He switched his mug to his other hand and wrapped her close to him.

"I know you've been praying, Caleb. So many other people have been too. Our ladies' group is meeting today to spend the day in prayer."

"I know, honey. I just don't get it. I feel like I am missing something."

"God's timing is perfect. He has a plan, you always tell me. So what is His plan? Are we to understand the mind of God? No, we're not. Jeremiah tells us that

159

His ways are not our ways and His thoughts not our thoughts." She paused.

Caleb waited. Over the years, he had learned his wife had a deep understanding of God, far deeper than he did. God had used her many times to provide answers. Would this be another one? She had with Laycee and Joshua.

Hannah looked at the sunrise brightening the eastern sky. This was a favourite time of the day for both of them, both early risers. This is when they knew they would have time for their couple's Bible study. Duties often came in later in the day and prevented that. She was trying to sort out her words. She knew God had spoken when she was reading His word this morning.

"I know you can't say much and never do. You have that integrity of a Godly man, my love. I have watched over the last few weeks. I have seen the struggles and the sorrows you have borne, not just for your friends but for your town." She tilted her head to look up at him. He was staring across the yard, listening intently to her words.

She continued. "I know you. You will find the answers. God has spoken to me, just like you know He does. There is a source in town for the contraband you are dealing with. This is the name God has given." She hesitated and then gave him the name.

Caleb stilled, then had to remember to breath. He closed his eyes and hugged his wife.

"Honey, I wish I had that connection with God you do. You certainly are a tool that He uses. Don't ever change. This name, this name. I don't know that I even would have considered it." They stood for a while longer, then as Hannah heard their boys up and ready for the day, they turned and walked back to the house.

Caleb strode into the office, a new light of determination on his face. Searching the room, he headed for both Ben and Eddie. "Come with me."

The men looked at each other and then at Caleb.

"Gather what you have and meet me in the conference room. I have a new lead."

Ben and Eddie were waiting for him when he entered, a stack of files on the table.

"Okay, before I give what I have, start a chart, Eddie." He tossed him a whiteboard marker.

Going through the files and sorting through the chain of evidence, a clear picture was emerging. They had one murder now they were sure were linked to the break-ins, possibly the second one.

Caleb stood back and studied the board. "We need to add Eric to that list. I think you'll find he was involved as well. He and David were pretty thick over the years, both into petty theft."

Ben and Eddie looked and then nodded. Eddie added the name.

"Walk me through it, Ben."

Ben walked them through what they had, the evidence they gathered.

"Okay. Now comes the fun part. You both love puzzles, I know. Give me your speculations and guesses and hunches. Eddie, you make a separate list."

They brainstormed for a while. Then Caleb walked to the board, took the marker from Eddie, and wrote one name down. The two men stared at it, stared at Caleb, and then stared at each other.

"It has to be Hannah again," Ben said and watched as Caleb smiled and nodded. "Where does she come up with these names? She was bang on with Laycee and Joshua. You didn't know, Eddie, that Hannah gave us a link to solve that case too."

"I know. It's a God thing she has going." Caleb smiled. "And I hope that God thing never stops.

"Eddie, it's your task to do leg work around town. Be cautious. He's had people killed. I don't want to attend an official police funeral.

"Ben, use your resources. But be as careful as you can. Having been in this town for so many years, who knows who he has in his pocket. Talk to your federal contacts. This will likely become a federal case for the smuggling, but we have murders and kidnappings on our books."

Both men left. Caleb studied the boards, pulled out his phone and snapped pictures of them, and then reached to wipe them clean. It would stay with just the three of them for now.

He stood and stared at the clean boards. "Lord," he prayed, "let this be the answer. Help us to solve this mystery. We need to find those two and soon. There needs to be healing in the families and in the town. With things unsolved, we just can't do that."

He turned. Liam was standing in the doorway behind him. Caleb went towards him and then directed him to the street. He needed time with his friend and his friend definitely needed time with him. Prayer would be the order of the day. The desk officer nodded as he left.

****

Leith stirred once more, eyes slowly opening. He didn't remember being awake before. Once again he studied the room. As his gaze moved around he saw Regan. He rolled to hands and knees, waiting for the spinning to stop, and then crawled over to her. He reached out a hand and breathed a sigh of relief. She was alive.

He sat back down and stared around, his mind working. How were they to get out of there? It looked a lot more solid than the last place. He stood, staggered as he caught his balance and then began a desperate search for an opening to get out. It was a solid room. He would never be able to chip through the wood, even if he had an axe, and he was pretty sure there wouldn't be one in the room. There was no garbage laying around this one. Whoever had set it up had made sure of that this time. The partitioned room had a toilet and sink. Leith stood at the doorway of that room and looked around. There was a fireplace at one end and cabinets on the wall. It looked like a cabin someone had been using over the winter, given the supply of logs stacked there. He searched the cupboards and they had been stripped of everything. He stopped by the windows. They had been boarded up but he just might be able to get one open. He checked. They had been nailed shut.

He heard a soft moan behind him and turned. Regan was stirring. He dropped back down beside her.

Regan moved, her head hurting with that movement. Where was she? It didn't feel like her bed. Her eyes moved and she focused. Leith's face swam into her view. She reached for his hand.

"Oh, thank God. You're awake. I don't know what I thought when I saw you earlier."

Leith studied her. "You were awake earlier?" At her nod, he spoke. "We need to try a find a way out of here. Are you up for that?"

She sat up slowly, finding this time there was no dizziness. "That I am." She thought a moment. "The two men were here. I know one of them but I can't think of his name."

"You know one of them?" At her nod, he looked around. "Okay. First we leave this place. Then we figure out how to get back home. Caleb will be able to help."

Both of them searched the room again. Regan finally stood in the centre and looked helplessly around.

"There is just no way, Leith. No way out. And I'm afraid that they will be back before we can escape."

"I'm going to find away." He stopped and searched the ceiling. Something had caught his eye. He moved towards the end where the sectioned off area was. "See there?" He pointed. "There, up in that corner. That's not a log. That's just plywood. And it looks as if it's been wet many times. That will soften it. I think if I can get it out, the hole will be big enough."

He pointed to the door. "Listen over there. If you hear anything, call."

Regan positioned herself by the door, and then watched, heart in throat, as Leith climbed logs to the area he was interested in.

He pushed and felt the wood give a bit. He looked down at Regan and she shook her head. He pushed again and this time wood fell away. He kept pushing and twisting, hanging on by his one elbow. Then the rest of the wood fell away. He was right. Regan would have no trouble getting out and he was sure he could get out by twisting and turning.

He dropped back to the floor and motioned Regan over. Whispering to her what he wanted to do, he took another search through the room. Feeling way back into a drawer, his hand touched something. He managed to pull it forward. A kitchen knife. Not real sharp but he was taking it with him.

Leith sent Regan up the wall, watching to make sure she didn't fall. She wiggled her way through and he heard a soft sound as she dropped to the ground. He wasted no time in scaling the wall and then dropping down beside her. The forest was a lot closer this time, just feet away. He grabbed for her hand and pulled her with him. A soft sound came to him and he spun, knife held ready. A dog appeared and he breathed a little easier. It was Betsy. Somehow she had followed and found them. He called her to them and then waited. No other sounds.

Then they heard the sound of a motor approaching. They needed to run but where? Leith grasped Regan's hand and turned into the forest. They were on a path they could follow for a while but they would need to find something else. He wasn't sure what kind of shape either one of them was in to keep running. Betsy followed at their heels, ears turned back and listening. She would warn them of danger. He needed to remember to thank her owner in a tangible way.

****

The King stepped out of the car and stretched. Finally, those two were locked up and he would be able to deal with them. Tonight would be it.

He motioned to the Knight who had been driving and sent him to unlock the door. The door swung open and hit the wall. The King stepped through. It was empty. The Knight followed and stared, mouth falling open. He strode to the bathroom area. Empty. He spun. They had been here six hours ago. Now they were gone.

The King's rage was intense. Not again. Not again. He was out of patience with everyone.

The Knight looked at him. "They were here. The door's locked. There is no way they could have gotten out."

"Well they did. You're responsible. Find them or you too will pay the price." Human lives no longer mattered to him.

The Knight searched the cabin and as his eyes raised, he saw the opening that Leith had created. Admiration for his determination to survive swept through him. He was a worthy opponent but one that would also succumb to his power.

The King swept from the room and back to the vehicle. The Knight closed the door and looked around. He would be back. He would get his gear and be back to track them. This time, they wouldn't make it back alive.

Chapter 15

Leith could feel Regan starting to lag. He looked around for a spot for them to rest.

"Over there." He pointed. He led her to a shaded area and helped her down. "Betsy will watch for us."

Regan rested her head on her knees. "I can't go on, Leith. I just don't have enough left to go on."

He was breathing heavy too. "We'll rest and then go on. We'll move slower. I think we're far enough away that we'll be okay. If it was them, chances are they aren't prepared to come in after us. They will have to go away and come back. Thing is, I just don't know how long that will take."

Regan raised her head and looked at him. "Still being the hawk, are you? You're watching for game, just like a hawk."

He smiled. That seemed to be her word for him.

"Okay. So what is that I see, Leith? There." She looked around. "That looks like it's in the south. Isn't that the tower from town, the one they used to have the bells in."

He squinted, then nodded. "It looks like it but it's so far away." He looked around and then pulled her to her feet. "Come on. We need to keep moving."

She reluctantly moved with him. "We need to find some water. There won't be anything to eat out here."

He nodded. "We will. Let's get as far as we can tonight. Maybe we'll be lucky and find someone we know."

Regan hesitated before speaking. "I don't know, Leith. How do we know who to trust? I know that voice. I just can't place it."

"It will come," he reassured her.

****

The Knights returned to the cabin. They had gathered what they needed. With first light, they would be on the search. This time, their prey would not escape. They did have admire their tenacity though, getting out of two locked buildings. But time was now of the essence. The King was very unhappy and he had let them know in no uncertain terms he wanted the situation dealt with. They didn't need to ask but they knew he was rolling up his business in town and getting ready to move on. To move with him, they needed to succeed.

****

Caleb moved quietly around the house, trying not to awaken any of his family. He couldn't sleep. His mind was trying to sort through so much information. He needed to think and couldn't.

He stepped outside and stopped. A dark figure sat on his deck. From the bit of light that was shining, he could see who it was and it was not who he expected.

He moved over and sat in silence. The silence continued but he made no effort to break it.

Finally the figure spoke. "I know where they are. And I know why. Can you help me if I help you?"

Caleb studied the figure. "You should have come to me before, Mark. Two of your friends are dead. What do you know?"

Mark Bell's head dropped. "I know. I wasn't here when that happened. Dad had me away at school." Mark's voice continued in a quiet manner as he detailed what he knew. Almost all of it, Caleb knew already.

"You say you know where they are?"

Mark nodded and gave an address.

Caleb stopped him. "No, Mark, that's not right. There is no such address and you know it. I want you to go with the officer standing behind you."

Mark jerked and looked around, a defeated look on his face. The officer helped him to his feet and walked away

Caleb sighed. Now what? This had the feeling of a set-up to get information. They had now brought it directly to his home and he didn't like it.

Morning came, and Caleb headed for Liam's house. He wasn't there and Caleb knew he had gone back to his work. He tracked him down in his office, asked some questions, and then left.

Liam's eyes followed Caleb as he walked away. What was the meaning of those questions?

Laycee appeared in his doorway next. She had come to spend time with him, and her work came with her. She settled down in a corner of his office and was soon engrossed in what she needed to accomplish with the therapy group she had been asked to lead. Joshua, she said, had gone to work as well. All of them felt they were in a holding pattern, a waiting game.

Liam looked down at his work. He needed to concentrate on the detailed drawing he was making and he just couldn't. He reached instead for his Bible.

****

Leith stirred in the dawning light. He listened and heard nothing. He looked at Regan who was still sleeping. He hadn't got much sleep, trying to keep watch, but his eyes had finally closed and he had slept. Betsy had crept between them, her body warmth spreading to both. She lay with her chin on his arm, intelligent brown eyes watching him. She was making him think twice about a dog. Maybe, when this was all over, he would look into one. He loved his sister's, Sheltie, Defiant, but had never really given much thought to a dog of his own. He sat up, thinking through the day They were getting closer to home but he needed to somehow find a food source for them. Water they could find but had nothing to carry it with them.

He reached over Betsy and roused Regan. She rubbed her eyes as she sat up. She was pale and tired and he could see her strength was waning. He needed to take care of her and he had no idea how that was even possible any more.

He grasped her hand and pulled her to her feet. With Betsy in front, they set off down the trail. Leith kept as close an eye as he could around them. He knew the dog would hear something well before he did and that warning he hoped would give them time to react and get to safety.

He looked up and asked for deliverance and safety. He still had no idea why they had been targeted but he hoped that Caleb had sorted it out.

Leith kept Regan moving as best he could, but he knew they couldn't go much further without proper food. He looked around. The area was getting more familiar they more they moved towards the south. If he remembered, there was a cabin near here somewhere, and that cabin was usually stocked with food and unlocked. It belonged to an older gentleman, a friend of his father's. He studied the sky and then veered their steps more to the west. Soon, he thought, they would find the cabin.

He had been right. There it was.

"Regan," he said as he pointed. "There's old man Jones' cabin. We'll find food and water there more than likely if he still stocks it."

Regan looked at the cabin, then her gaze shot around. "How do we know it's safe?"

"Betsy. I'll let her go in ahead of us. She'll alert if anything's around. They won't harm her, if they're there. They'll want her for tracking."

Regan's eyes closed. "Please, let there be no one around. I need some food."

Betsy headed for the cabin at Leith's command. Sniffing around, she circled the cabin, then came back and faced them, tail wagging slowly. It was safe, at least for the moment.

They made their way to the building. Leith tucked Regan behind him and slowly opened the door. Betsy entered, sniffed around and came back out. Leith breathed a sigh of relief. Now, if the cabin was as he remembered it, they could get some food and get away again.

Regan sank down onto the easy chair. It felt good to sit in a chair instead of on the ground. Leith was rummaging in the cupboards and brought her some trail mix he had found.

"Eat this. I don't want to start a fire. It would give us away. I'm going to pack up some stuff to take with us."

Regan dug into her pocket and pulled out some bills. "Here. Leave this somewhere so he'll find it." Leith turned as she spoke. "I always tuck money in my pockets, just in case."

He smiled. "That's good to know. Smart thinking."

They quickly packed up what they needed in a knapsack Leith unearthed. He knew he would be able to return it at some point.

With Betsy in the lead, they once more made their way towards the south. The tower was getting closer. Now that he was in more familiar territory, he would be able to pick the trails that would move them in a quicker manner to town.

Coming to the edge of a road, Leith stopped. He could hear a car coming and drew Regan back. It was a forestry vehicle, moving slowly. Leith ducked his head to see who it was and recognized a friend. He stepped out and waved down the vehicle. A quick explanation, and they were in the vehicle on their way to town and back to their families.

The two Knights halted and watched the vehicle pull away. They had been so close, just like so many times. Another failure. How many would there be before they succeeded?

Chapter 16

Eddie tapped at Caleb's office door and entered. Ben was already sitting there, file folders open in front of him.

"So, where do we stand now?" Caleb asked.

Ben spoke, shuffling through the papers. "I'm still waiting for some of the financial information to come back from my contact, but it looks as he's been putting money away for years overseas. It runs into the millions. There is no way he has made that much money with the legitimate business."

Eddie nodded. "That's what I'm finding too. Word is getting around on the street that if you want work, you contact him. And it's not for sweeping and cleaning. He's becoming violent. I don't know how much longer he'll stay controlled enough to be able to enter normal company."

Caleb leaned back and thought. "We need to keep up the pressure. When they searched the homes and store, did they find anything?"

Ben handed over a sheet. "This is a detailed report of what they found. Five crates had that mark and we pulled at low estimate three million just in uncut stones. They would be worth much more than that once cut and set."

Caleb whistled. "I guess that explains why the desperation. Let's keep digging." He paused as his phone rang. He dug it out and glanced at the number. The hospital. His heart sank at the thought it was one of his sons.

"Logan." He answered, a professional tone in his voice to cover his fear. As he listened, his eyes widened and his gaze shot to the two men sitting in front of them. Ben and Eddie both straightened, knowing something was happening. "Thank you. We're on our way."

Caleb returned his phone to his pocket as his eyes slid shut in thanks. Opening them, he gesturing for the two to follow him.

Without a word, they locked up the files and then ran for the door.

Once in Caleb's vehicle, he turned. "That was the hospital. Leith and Regan were found about an hour ago by a forestry worker. They're safe. He took them to the hospital."

"They're safe but we still need to arrange protection until we can bring that fellow down," Ben commented. "It's going to be very hard to do that."

Eddie nodded in agreement. "We'll come up with a plan. Thing is, how long do we have and will he try again?"

"You can be sure he'll try again." Caleb pulled into the parking at the hospital and turned off his vehicle. "We need to be ready. Before we go in, let's take a minute. Ben, keep pushing those financials. Eddie, keep working the streets. I'll arrange for protection for them, but I have a feeling Regan's Dad is already taking that step. Our job will be to bring this investigation to as quick a close as we can."

Caleb strode into the Emergency Department followed by Ben and Eddie. Eddie headed for the waiting room where the families had gathered. Right now, he would be the protection they needed. Who knew what the next step would be and he had a bad feeling that the families would become a target.

Caleb stopped and spoke with the clerk and then headed further back. He motioned Ben to where Regan was and he stepped into the room where Leith was laying on the stretcher. He stopped beside his friend and watched his face. Leith's eyes were closed. The trauma of the last few days was written on his face in the mud, the scratches, the bruises. He could see the fatigue in the gauntness of his face, the dark circles under his eyes. He raised his eyes and traced the IV line running to Leith's wrist. Questioning could wait. Leith needed to sleep.

He stepped out of the room and found Ben waiting, two officers standing behind him. Caleb motioned for them to take positions at the doorways and then moved away with Ben.

"How is she?"

"Rough. They had a pretty bad time of it I would say. She didn't say much, but she is angry. I'll question her later on what happened. How's Leith?"

"He's sleeping right now. He's in rough shape I would say. The doctors are keeping them overnight?"

"That's my understanding. You'll want men posted the whole time, I gather."

Caleb nodded. "Absolutely. We'll need to get some answers from them and then work from there. The families are in the waiting room?"

"Yes. Eddie's with them. They may well become a target if these two can't be reached. It's going to be a real fine line we have to tread."

"Don't I know it."

After spending a night in hospital, both Leith and Regan were discharged. Caleb was waiting for them as they came through the lobby, surrounded by their families. He looked up at the ceiling, then back down to them.

"Okay, this is what we're doing." He glanced up, eyes narrowing as he studied a man standing near the coffee shop. Word was out and he knew he had to race against time to protect these two. "You're not going to your home, only long enough for you to collect what you need. These officers will be going with you," as he indicated the officers standing beside them. "Your families will be tucked away somewhere as well. Neither one of you will be safe until this ends and I want it to end well."

Leith started to protest but Caleb cut him off. "I have taken the liberty of speaking with the homeowner. He understands the situation and is adamant that he wants you safe and sound. He told me he couldn't find another two tile setters he would work with." A small smile cracked Caleb's face. "I agree with him."

Regan stood in her bedroom and looked around. She had gathered up what she needed but she wasn't ready to leave. Her mother came up behind her, turned her around and hugged her. The family had been through so much tragedy in the last few weeks. Regan's tears soaked her mother's sweater, then with a final hug, she stepped back.

"I'll be okay, Mom," she whispered. "I'll be okay."

Her mother reached and tucked auburn hair away from Regan's eyes. "I know, baby, I know, but I just want you here. I understand." Her mother then clasped her hands with Regan's and bowed, asking for guidance, wisdom and protection.

"You be safe, Mom, you and Dad. I couldn't bear it if something happened to you."

Regan turned, grabbed her knapsack, and descended the stairs to where her father stood. A quick hug and Ben had whisked her out the door. He studied the area, confident they weren't being watched, tucked Regan in his car, and pulled away. Now to take the next step.

Liam stood and watched his brother's back. Leith looked beat up and tired, but determined. Laycee stood beside him, hand on her mouth and tears in her eyes, Joshua's arm around her.

Leith said not a word, didn't go near his family. This was unusual for him. They were close and never left one another without a word or a hug. As he passed Liam, Liam's hand on his shoulder stopped him. He waited until with a soft grip,

Liam's dropped his hand.   Laycee's hand reached for his, he clasped it quickly and then walked out to where Caleb was waiting, determination in each step.   This had hit at his home and his friends and he would stop at nothing to end it.

Caleb watched Leith walk towards him and noted the change in him.   He nodded.   His friend was ready to fight, and he would help him.   Now to get him to safety.

****

The King glared at the one Knight standing in front of him.   "YOU IMBECILE!" he yelled. "How did they get away from you again?   Are you that incompetent?"

The Knight stared back, no longer afraid.   "No, we are not that incompetent. We have being doing our very best. Someone had to be helping them escape, that is the only explanation."

"If that's the case, then who is it and where is he?   Find him and bring him to me." The voice shook crystal on the shelves and rattled vases sitting on display.

The Knight turned and left, this time without being dismissed. Was it really worth it, this job? He hadn't been part of the murders but he would bear a penalty the same. He really had to think this through. He heard the sound of breaking glass from behind the door and was glad he was not in that room.

Chapter 17

Regan dropped her bag on the bed in the room she had been assigned and looked around. It was a small room, with a bed, dresser, and easy chair along with the table by the bed. There was a small closet beside her and when she walked over to the door on the opposite wall, it opened up into a small compact bathroom. She laid her head on the door frame. That was such a blessing. She so needed to get clean but first she needed to find Leith, to make sure he was okay. She left the room and headed down the hall to the kitchen.

Caleb and Ben turned as she came in and hesitated.

"Come on in, Regan. Ben's got some soup and sandwiches ready. You need to eat and then get some sleep."

She nodded but made no move to walk forward. "Where's Leith?"

"He's getting settled." Caleb studied her, walked over to her and turned her around. "Food can wait. You're almost asleep on your feet. Go. Get some sleep. We'll talk when you awake."

Caleb watched as she walked back down the hall, one hand out to touch the wall and keep her balanced. He shook his head. He so wanted to find the man responsible for the whole situation. He turned back to kitchen and met Ben's eyes. Both knew that they weren't done and who knew what the next few days would bring.

"I'm going to check on Leith," Ben said as he passed him. "I thought he would be out here by now."

Ben returned. "He's asleep. The best thing for those two. I can't even begin to imagine what they've been through."

Caleb nodded from where he sat at the table. "I know. God protected them for sure." He sighed, then continued, "What do we have? Any closer?"

Ben shook his head. "No. I've pulled everything I have. It's not enough. We don't have enough for a warrant to search the premises, let alone arrest him."

Caleb ran his hand through his hair. "We'll need to come up with something. We have to end this in the next few days. Those two can't take much more."

Ben agreed, then was silent as they ate. They would be there for the duration as well. Their families understood.

It was early evening before Leith finally surfaced. He looked around and then remembered. They were still trapped, trapped at the whim of the maniac after them. Until he was found, they wouldn't be free or safe. He let his head drop back on the bed. He had to come up with a plan to succeed, only he had no idea who he needed to succeed against. He was here, cut off from his family at a time he needed them. He rose, grabbed a quick shower and clean clothes and headed to find something to eat.

Caleb turned from the counter where he had been making a mug of tea. Leith stared at him and then turned to get some coffee.

"There're sandwiches in the fridge. Soup is hot on the stove."

Leith nodded his thanks as he grabbed some food and then sat at the worn table in the kitchen. He had no idea where he was but God did. God provided another tower for them to hide in. Please, God, let this be it. Let this tower protect.

Caleb set his mug on the table across from him and pulling out a chair, sat.

"How's Regan?" Leith asked.

"She's still sleeping. I checked on her a while ago. She may well sleep through the night."

Caleb studied his friend. "What aren't you telling me?"

Leith paused in his chewing and then continued to eat. How could he explain his feelings and his thoughts? They were still so muddled in his mind, they didn't make sense.

"I'm so muddled in my thoughts, Caleb, I don't know where to begin. I gave you my statement but I feel like I'm missing something."

Caleb stood, grabbed a pad of paper and a pen and sat back down. "Start talking. Just talk. I'll write. We can sort through it later. Start with your day away."

Leith began talking and Caleb began writing. Page after page was turned. Finally, Leith stopped, exhausted. He laid his head on his crossed arms and almost sobbed.

"I couldn't stop them. I couldn't protect her."

Caleb watched, sympathy on his face. "We can't always. That's what we are trying to do now. Let me go through what you said here and we'll see what we have that's added to what you first gave us."

"Let me help." A voice from the door caught their attention. Regan stood there, then came and sank down in another chair at the table. Leith arose and found food and coffee for her, placing them in front of her.

"Let me tell what I remember. There will be differences. Maybe combining the two will help."

Caleb again filled page after page of notes. When Regan stopped, he looked up. "Okay. I'm going to find Ben."

Leith reached for Regan's hand and touched it. She drew back. She stood and with her back to him said, "No, Leith. I can't." Sobs in her voice rocked him as he watched her run from the room and heard the sound of her door closing. Hands on the back of his neck, he looked up and then back down. This had to end.

Early the next morning, an exhausted Caleb sat back. He and Ben had spent the night going through the pages they had. It was making sense. It was giving them more and more information that would help them to stop this.

"Do you think Regan will remember who the voice is?" Ben questioned.

"In a way, I hope she does. In a way, I hope she doesn't. That's a dangerous spot for her. If somehow word gets out, that it's done for her. Her family will likely suffer too." Caleb stood and paced. "I just don't know, Ben. I just don't know. Guess I'm getting too tired."

"Go grab some sleep. We have men here to watch."

"Thanks. Wake me in a couple of hours."

Leith grabbed another mug of coffee and sat back down at the table, lost in thought.   He startled at a hand on his shoulder and looked up.

Eddie stood there, then moved to grab a mug of his own. He sat back down at the table and watched Leith.   He could the exhaustion and strain in his face.

"What's up, Leith?"

Leith shook his head. "Nothing."

Eddie smiled, then spoke, "No, something is up other than why you're here. What is it?"

Leith looked up and then said, "It's Regan. I just don't understand."

Eddie smiled again and said, "She's a woman.   You're not meant to understand. Seriously though, she's been through a lot in the last few weeks. Abducted twice, taking on a new job after moving home, losing an uncle and then a cousin. Give her time."

Leith shook his head. "I can but I just don't want to lose her again."

"What do you mean, again?"

"She left 10 years ago as soon as we graduated. I was getting ready to ask her out and then she was gone. Now she's back and more beautiful than ever, not just in looks. She's working for me and I have to be so careful. This isn't how I planned it 10 years ago."

Eddie laughed and Leith looked at him in surprise. "Nothing ever goes as we plan it, you should know that, Leith. God is the author of our days, not us." He paused and studied his hands. "I'm going to tell you a story from long ago. Just listen, okay. One day there was a young man in love with a beautiful young woman. They were friends but he wanted her to be a permanent part of his life. She suddenly left town without saying why. He was hurt. When she returned a couple of years later, he tried to get close and she wouldn't let him. Finally, he was able to break through the barriers she had erected around herself, find out what was going on. Their love grew and they married and started a family. It was not an easy road they chose to walk, but God led them through each twist and turn."

Leith studied Eddie and listened as he spoke. "So what are you saying?"

"Give her time. Be her friend. Treat her with care and respect. Stay within the boundaries she has set up to protect her heart. The day will come when she will talk to you and you to her. You're still young. You've got time." Eddie rose and went to set his mug in the sink. As he walked by Leith, his hand came out and he laid it on Leith's black hair as if in a benediction. "Those two young people I told you about? You know them very well. They were your parents."

Leith spun to stare after Eddie. He had never known that. He wondered if Liam or Laycee did, but doubted it. His parents never spoke of early days. He knew Eddie and his parents had been long time friends but didn't know he had history of them the family had never known. He would need to get to know Eddie better.

Chapter 18

Caleb stopped at the department. He needed to get a sense of what else was going on. He stopped and spoke with each officer, finding out where they stood in their duties, and offering words of encouragement.

Entering his office, he sank wearily into his chair and looked at the paperwork his secretary had stacked there for him. He reached for the top folder and dug in to clear as much as he could. He needed sleep but this needed to be done before that.

Hours later he looked up at a tap at his door. Hannah stood there. She walked over to him and into his embrace. Hugging him for a minute, she then leaned back.

"You're tired, Caleb."

He nodded. "I am. I'm also....also...." He stopped, at a loss for words.

Hannah laughed. "It's not often that you can't express yourself. Here, take this. Read it after I'm gone." With a quick kiss, she left.

With a sense of foreboding, Caleb shut his office door and sat down again. He studied the piece of notepaper his wife had handed him. He closed his eyes and opened them again. It was still there. Wishful thinking wouldn't make it disappear.

He slowly unfolded it and read the name she gave him. His eyes closed. Not who he expected. He searched the room, looking for answers or a way to stop the insane ride they all were on. Nothing was there. He reached over to the paper shredder and watched as the paper disappeared. For now, the name remained with him.

He bent back to his paperwork, the name running through his mind. Once he had cleared his desk, he stood. He was headed home for a while and then back to the house where they had stashed Leith and Regan.

****

The King stood once again in front of the window, hands behind his back. His empire was crumbling faster than he thought possible. He had lost underlings and he didn't even know if he could still trust his Knights. His sources on the street were either no longer available to him or could not or would not give him much information. He needed to find those two and eliminate them. But where were they? They had made it back alive and now were hidden. He couldn't get to their families, they too had been hidden away. Somehow, some way, he would succeed.

****

Leith was tired. He was tired of running. He was tired of hiding. He was tired of not knowing who or why. Caleb and Ben weren't saying much and the officers guarding them were tight-lipped. He turned to watch Regan. She was showing the strain but had found a library tucked away in a room and had curled up in a chair to read. The sunlight reflected off her auburn hair and turned highlights to gold. He reached for paper. He might as well put some of his design thoughts down. Had it only been that short a time since they had wandered through that town, laughing and plotting designs?   He was soon engrossed in his work.

He looked up as he heard the door and Caleb and Ben walked in. The serious look on their faces made his heart rise to his throat and then plummet. His first thought was that something had happened to Liam or Laycee.

"Leith, can you join us here?" Caleb asked.

He sank down on the couch near Laycee's chair. She had lowered her book and was staring at the two. He could see that she was thinking the same as he had.

Caleb stood in front of the fireplace and warmed his hands at the low fire burning. Ben had gone to stand in the kitchen door.

Caleb turned, leaned his arm on the mantle and rested his head for a minute. Raising his head, his eyes searched the two in front of him.

"We have made some progress. Not enough yet to let you go home or for your families to go home. I'm not telling you where they are and they don't know where you are." He paused, drew in a breath before continuing. "I have been given a name and I want to give it to you. Think very carefully before you respond. I will not tell you how I got it. Before you respond to it, again think over your dealings with this person."

He studied them again as he waited. They exchanged puzzled glances and then returned their eyes to him.

"George White."

Leith's eyebrows drew together as he mulled over that name. He remembered him from his high school class but hadn't seen him since graduation. He had no idea if George was still in town.

Regan's gasped, drawing all eyes to her. "That's him." She turned to Leith. "That's the voice I heard. Oh, no!" Hands flew to her mouth and she paled. "He was friends with David. Did he have something to do with David's death?"

Caleb crouched before her and reached for her hands. "We don't know, Regan. We don't know. We are trying to locate George but he has hidden himself well over the years. We'll find him."

Regan's eyes filled with tears and she reached for some tissue.

"What can you tell about him?" Caleb keen eyes searched her face, taking in the shock that she had just received.

"Sit, Caleb." She motioned for him to sit down. "I have a tale to tell and may be if I had told it earlier nothing would have happened."

She hesitated, then stopped. "I can't, I just can't." She sprang from her chair and ran to her room, shutting the door behind her.

Leith stood as if to go after her, then hesitated. Anguished eyes met Caleb's sympathetic ones.

"Let her go, Leith. She needs time."

"So what are you not telling me?"

"George has always been outside the law, you will agree? For the last five to seven years, we have known contraband has been sliding through our town. George was fingered as one to watch. He has pretty much disappeared and yet the smuggling continues. Small stuff that's easy to hide, but which brings in a lot of money. We know there is someone here is town masterminding it but we don't have the proof we need. We're getting close."

Ben spoke up. "What you two have dug up for us through your adventures has helped. I don't think you realize how much information you two stored away. Impressions, voices, etc."

Leith shook his head. "I don't care about that. I care about her and I want her safe."

"So do we, Leith. So do we. Her family and your family want you both safe and that's what we're trying to do. In the next day or so, we will have to move you both again, just because this may be a compromised site."

Leith looked up at that. "So you're saying you have a mole in your department?"

Caleb shook his head. "No. But there is more traffic than normal coming here. Someone will notice and say something to someone who will say something to someone else, and the snowball starts and doesn't stop."

Ben added, "By tomorrow, we'll have another place ready for you and you'll move. Your families are safe."

Leith leaned back. "I am so tired of it all."

Caleb and Ben had to agree. They would be glad when everything was back to as normal as it ever got.

****

Liam turned from the window he had been looking out and sighed. He wanted his life back, he wanted his family to have their lives back. He watched Laycee as she paced, frustration in her every move.

"When, Liam? When do we get to go home?"

"I don't know, Laycee. Soon I hope. I just pray that Leith and Regan are okay. We're not getting told to protect all of us."

Laycee stopped her pacing and rested her gaze on him. Then her shoulders dropped as she gave into the thought. "I know. I really do know. I just wish..." She let her voice drop away. They both wished for the same thing.

Joshua stood watching them both, hurting for them and in particular for his fiancee. He knew she was really hurting and was learning how to trust God in a whole new way. He was too. He reached for her and gathered her close. His eyes met Liam's over her head and they agreed. Whatever it took, they would do to bring their families back together.

Chapter 19

Morning came, and Regan zipped up the backpack, checking to make sure she had everything. Caleb was moving them again and she had no idea where. She was tired and just wanted her own bed. Who knew when that would happen?

She entered the living room and stood, dejection in her manner. Leith's heart broke as he watched her. He so wanted to protect her and sooth her worries, but he couldn't. He just couldn't.

Caleb came in through the door, phone to his ear. Ben stood waiting in the kitchen doorway, Eddie on the porch. Caleb finished his call and then pocketed his phone. His keen eyes searched the group and then turned to watch the outdoors. He didn't feel right about this. Something felt all wrong. He had learned to trust his instincts.

Ben caught his eye and motioned with his head. Caleb and he stood in the kitchen talking. The others couldn't hear what was being said but knew something was up.

Caleb returned to the room.

"This is what we're going to do. Leith and Regan, you're with Ben. Stay tight with him.

"Eddie, we need to clear this place, to return it to what it was. That's your job." Caleb stared at him.

Eddie stared back, then caught on to what Caleb was meaning. He nodded. "No problem."

"Let's go, people."

Leith and Regan slid into Ben's car and he drove away. A couple of miles down the road he turned onto the side road and then continued for just a couple of more miles. He pulled off into a laneway and waited. The car was hidden from view. About 30 minutes later, a black car passed them going in the same direction as they had been headed. Ben pulled back onto the road and returned the way he had come, back to the cabin. Caleb and Eddie were waiting.

Ben rolled down his window. "Black Lexus, this is the plate and year."

Caleb drew a deep breath and looked over the car at Eddie. "You were right. We have a leak somewhere."

Regan and Leith exchanged glances. A leak and who? Where their families safe?

Ben turned in his seat. "Guess you heard, eh? We're down to just us three looking after you two. We'll keep you safe."

Regan spoke. "Get me a gun."

Leith turned to stare at her as did the others.

"Get me a gun. I have a permit to carry but don't have my gun with me. Get me a gun. I'm trained."

"Very interesting, young lady." Ben's tone was amused. "And when were you planning on telling us something we already knew?"

Regan smiled. "I gathered you did. It's not something I like to talk about. Things happened and I needed to break away from that. I'm still not sure I can shoot someone."

"If we need to, we will."   Caleb looked around.   "For now, we need to get you out of sight.   This place has been compromised as well, from what Eddie says."

Eddie held up the bag he was holding. "Bugs and not the kind that bite."

Leith laid his head back on the seat.   "I hope you guys know what you're doing because it sure is beginning to feel like you're 10 steps behind."

Caleb leaned down to look through the window.   "We do.   Ben is taking you down the road to another vehicle and then we're off, just like Dorothy in the Wizard."

Regan shook her head.   "Caleb, your age is showing.   Are you reading that to your boys or spending time watching it?"

Caleb laughed at her and then hit the roof of the car for Ben to move off.   He and Eddie stood watching.

"I have a bad feeling, boss," Eddie commented.

"I know.   So do I."

Ben turned into an older home in a part of town they were not familiar with.   He hit the remote to open the garage and then closed the door once the car was inside. He turned.

"Being in town brings a few new rules. This place has been closed up looking for years. It has been kept that way, as if the owner is just away on vacation. It is clean inside although the furniture is sparse. We have you on the main floor, just for safety's sake. When we go inside, I will run you through the escape routes we have set up. Learn them. Your life may well depend on them."

Regan's frightened eyes met Leith's. They still weren't safe. Why was God letting this happen? The faith she had depended on for her bedrock of life felt like it was starting to slip.

Leith took her hand as they entered the house, his grip strong and steady. They followed Ben as he took them through what they needed to know. He really hoped they never did need to use them, but somehow someone kept finding them.

For now they would be safe. But for how long?

****

Eddie tapped, then entered Caleb's office, closing the door. Caleb looked up and at Eddie's nod, his eyes slid shut. He had been afraid of this and had hoped it wasn't true. Eddie had confirmed their suspicions.

"All right, Eddie. You know what to do."

Eddie left and then returned with the department's younger secretary, Susan. Caleb studied her and then indicated she should have a seat.

Susan sat and waited. She shifted uncomfortably as the silence grew.

"Why, Susan? Why the betrayal?" Caleb voice was soft and composed, belying the anger that raged inside him.

"Why, what, Chief? I don't know what you're talking about."

Eddie bent over her shoulder from behind and starting laying documents and notes down into her hands. Her face paled as she saw each one, saw that they had tracked her through everything she had done in the last year.

"Why, Susan?"

Her rage exploded. "I never get the credit for my research. I never get acknowledged. This is a dead end job with no room to grow. I want more from life. I want more, just more."

"You knew when you hired on what the job entailed." Caleb stopped and then stood. "We are going to spare you the humiliation of being incarcerated in this jail. Eddie will take you to the conference room. Your purse and jacket are there. From there, officers from Oak City will escort you to their jail. You will be arraigned first on federal charges of smuggling, and then the list of charges will grow."

"You'll never find who you're looking for. He's too well hidden." She spit the words at him.

"We already know, Susan, we already know. Our case is just about built."

She stopped, shocked at the words. Before she could say anything else, Eddie escorted her away in a quiet manner that drew no attention.

Caleb sat back down and rubbed his neck. Eddie came back and shut the door, handing Caleb a mug of tea as he sat down in a chair in front of the desk.

"We'll need a cover story. She can't just disappear without someone asking."

Caleb nodded. "I hate this part of the job, Eddie, finding out one of our own is involved. It leaves a bitter, bitter taste."

"That it does. I just hope she's the only one. It would really hurt if she isn't."

"You've delved into her background?"

"I have. There were no red flags at first until I started more digging. She had been married, divorced and was using her maiden name. Her married name is Brand. Husband was Eric. She had hidden that well. It's almost as if she had help at the court house to do so."

"Now that's a scary thought, Eddie. I don't even want to think about that one."

"Me neither, Chief. Listen I'm headed off the night. Take some time too. Ben will call if he needs us."

"I intend to spend some time at home with Hannah and the boys. Ben will give an update later. Have a good night."

Eddie raised his hand as he left.

Caleb stretched and then closed and locked away the files he had been working on. He didn't need anyone seeing the case until he was ready for them. After Susan's betrayal, his trust level just wasn't there. He turned the light out in his office, caught up his briefcase and made his way out of the department.

Chapter 20

Regan stretched and then reached for her Bible. All was quiet in the house. She didn't know how Ben kept going, being the only one. She just so wanted to see her parents and couldn't. Soon, she hoped, and she opened her Bible to read through favourite passage of comfort.

Leith stood at the counter, restlessly tapping his finger as he waited for the coffee. He was getting frustrated at no activity. He wanted to go back to his life. He wanted to see what would happen with Regan, who he wanted as a permanent part of his life.

Ben grabbed the coffee pot from in front of him. "If you snooze, you lose, boy?"

Leith laughed and held out his mug. "Here, you pour. You've got the pot."

Ben laughed as well. "Caleb says he found our leak at the department. They are hopeful that it's only the one."

Leith turned and looked at him, eyes moving over as he saw Regan in the doorway. "Who was it?"

Ben shook his head. "Not telling. You'll find out when we get it all sorted out. In the meanwhile, he's afraid this place has been compromised as well. Drink your coffee and then grab your stuff. He's lining up another place."

Regan turned. "No, no coffee for me. I can't handle it. I can't handle another move."

Leith turned to go after her. Ben's hand on his arm stopped him. "Be patient with her, Leith. She's hurting in ways neither one of us can imagine."

Leith nodded and then followed Regan. He stood at the door watching her pack.

"I'm tired of it too, Regan. I want time with my family. I want my life back, to go back to the quiet tasks of planning and laying tile. We'll get there. We just need…"

She turned and her anger flared. "We just need what, Leith? Just what is it?"

The sound of a breaking door and Ben's surprised yell startled them. Leith grabbed for Regan's hand and pulled her down the hall to the back bedroom. He shut and locked the door, then turned finger on her mouth. "Quiet. We need to get away. Come on." He led her to the closet and then pushed on the panel Ben had shown them. Shoving her through, he slid the panel back into place. It was very dark and he didn't a light. He caught her hand and pulled her down the steps and then along a low damp space. Ben had thought it might have been from smugglers long ago as they were close to the river. He had no idea where it would come out but he wasn't waiting around to find out who was there. He said a quick prayer for Ben that he was all right.

"There are boards, Leith. Is it safe to move them?"

Leith stopped and listened, then carefully pulled one away, then a second one. He pulled her with him. They were in a shed, Leith figured at the back of the property. He cautiously pulled the door open and peeked out. So far, so good. He crept out, Regan right behind him. They followed the wall until they could reach the back fence and then push out the boards Ben had told them would move. They went on as silent feet as they could towards the next street.

Sirens sounded behind them. Help was on the way but they wouldn't go back. They had to move forward. A sound in front of them stopped them and they looked up. A black-garbed man stood in front of them, arm raised, revolver pointed at them. Leith pushed Regan aside and leapt for the gunmen. A muffled sound and Leith fell. Regan screamed and ran towards him. Another sound and she was down.

The gunman walked forward and stood over them, then turned and walked away. The Knight had completed his task. The job was ended and he could go on with his life.

****

Caleb shoved the door to his car open and revolver drawn ran cautiously to the open door of the house, Eddie at his heels. Scanning the area, they moved into the house, officers spreading out to surround it. Caleb's heart sank when he saw Ben's crumpled form. Eddie stooped and then nodded. Ben was alive. They quickly cleared the house. There was no sign of Leith or Regan.

Caleb stared around, then turned to Eddie. "There's an escape route. If I remember, it ends at the shed. Come on."

The two turned and raced for the backyard, praying they were in time. Sudden shouts sounded from the other side of the fence and then gunfire. Their hearts were in their mouths as they pushed through the fence and ran down the road.

Caleb skidded to a stop. Two forms lay close together, almost touching. Raising his eyes, he could see officers handcuffing a man in black. Caleb approached the two bodies. Leith and Regan. "Please Lord, let us be in time."

Eddie has bending over Regan. "She's alive but just barely."

Caleb felt for a pulse. "Leith is alive too. Get the paramedics in here."

Caleb stood back and watched as the paramedics worked on his two friends. Movement beside him made his turn. Ben was standing there, bandage on his head.

"You should be at the hospital, Ben."

Ben shook his head and then grimaced. "Not until they go. Not until then." He squinted against the light. "Eddie says they got the gun man."

Caleb nodded. "George White."

Ben thought about that and then said, "It fits with him. It really does." He stopped as more commotion came from where Leith and Regan lay. Leith had been moved to a stretcher and being wheeled to a waiting ambulance. The paramedics were frantically working on Regan and Caleb's heart fell when he saw the paramedics desperately trying to stop the bleeding. He prayed she made it. He watched as she was loaded onto a stretcher and raced to a waiting ambulance, as the race to save her life continued. He looked around.

Eddie was ahead of him, already in a cruiser ready to lead the rush to the hospital. Ben and Caleb stood watching, hearts in mouths, and prayers on their lips.

"Send some officers to bring their families to the hospital. Just say they've been hurt and they've been taken there. We'll deal with what we have to when we get there. Then get yourself there."

Ben nodded and walked away, shoulders slumped from more than pain. The blow to his head was hard enough to handle but knowing he hadn't be able to save them just added to his burden.

Caleb made his rounds with the investigators and crime scene team. They would be busy for a while. He knew they would get to him with what they had as soon as they could.

He turned and scanned the area, still feeling like he was being watched. It's not over yet, he though, not yet. Eyes lifting to heaven, he once again prayed for his friends.

He slid behind the wheel of his car and inserted the key into the ignition, then sat back. Something was still niggling at the back of his mind. He shrugged. It would come, he supposed, when he least expected it.

Chapter 21

Ben met Caleb outside the hospital. He had had his head examined and besides being told he had a hard head, just that he needed to rest and take his pain medications. He had no concussion. He stared ahead of him as Caleb stopped beside him, fearing the worse.

"The families are in the waiting room at the back. The officers cleared it and set up security there. It's the easier way to watch them."

"How are Leith and Regan?"

"I think they've taken Leith to surgery already. He was hit in shoulder, but they don't think it's done much damage. He's a very fortunate young man. It shouldn't affect his work once he's healed."

"And Regan?"

Ben didn't comment and Caleb's heart sunk again. "I haven't heard much, other than that she's still alive. It was really touch and go on the ride over. They almost lost her a couple of times." He paused, then turned to look at Caleb. "It just isn't fair, Caleb. A beautiful young woman like that, targeted because of some greedy crazy, and she almost dies. The bullet hit her chest, really near the heart. They're taking her to surgery, but they won't know until they get in if the heart has been damaged. She may not come through surgery, may not even make it to the Operating Room."

Caleb didn't speak. His emotions, usually under strong control, were getting the best of him. "We'll pray her through, Ben. Knowing the pastor's wife, she already has the prayer chain working."

Ben nodded towards the door. "The pastor is in there with them."

Caleb took a deep breath and faced the door. His head moved and he looked up at the sky that was starting to darken for night. "Nothing we train for ever really prepares you for this. It's been a long few days. Where's Eddie? "

"He headed back to the department. He said he wanted to make sure everything is by the book."

Caleb nodded and then stepped forward. Nothing ever prepared him for this. He would never ever get used to times like this.

He nodded at the officer at the door to the waiting room and entered, eyes searching. Hannah saw him and rushed to him. He held his wife, drawing from her strength. She didn't have to speak, he could hear what she was saying.

His gaze rose and connected with Liam. Liam headed for him. Hannah moved to one side. Liam stopped in front of Caleb, unable to speak, emotions too high to control. His brown eyes were shiny with tears that he refused to let fall. He reached and drew Caleb into a bear hug.

Liam stood back, hands on Caleb's arm, unable to speak. He clapped his friend's arm and then turned away.

Laycee stood there, Joshua's arm around her. Caleb reached for the two and hugged them. Laycee's face was wet, but there was a peace there. Caleb hoped he

225

could find that peace but he wasn't sure any more that he could.

He then paced to where Regan's parents sat and squatted down in front of her mother. She reached and touched his face.

"I know, Caleb, I know. You're hurting. You feel like you failed. You didn't. You kept them as safe as you could in this evil world. You kept them in a strong tower for as long as you could. You did your best. God led you. He is in control. Let it go."

Caleb bowed his head. He felt unworthy of their words. He felt a hand on his head. Joseph Evans was reaching out too, in the midst of his own grief and worry. He didn't hear the words that were prayed, but a sense of peace began to filter through him.

He stood, eyes clearing and looked around. He walked over to Ben and Eddie. His eyes drifted past them and stopped. How dare he come here and watch? Caleb dropped his eyes again. He murmured something to them and they turned. The man had left.

"See if we can get set up in here something to go over what we have. I don't want to leave." Caleb looked around. "I just need to be here with my friends, I need to be myself, a hurting friend, not the chief for a few minutes."

"We'll look after it," Ben said. "Eddie has brought the files you wanted. We'll come find you."

Caleb stood, lost in thought. There was still something he was missing.

"What are you missing, Caleb?" Liam stood beside him. Caleb's friend knew him well, knew he would puzzle away at the problem like Defiant with his knuckle bone, until he reached the answer.

"I wish I knew, Liam. There's something, and I know Regan has the key. She started to say something once and stopped. She said she couldn't continue. Then she asked for a gun, said she had a permit and that something had happened where she was living. I wish I had been able to get those answers."

"I wish I could help. Even Laycee, who kept in touch, has no idea why she left or what went on. Have you talked to her parents?"

Caleb turned to look at them. "No, but I am going to have to." He reached for the cup of tea Joshua was handing him. "Any more word yet?"

Joshua shook his head. "They said it would be quite a while. We'll be here for hours yet."

"Make sure you all get something to eat. You'll need it."

"You too, brother." Joshua moved away to Laycee.

****

Caleb stood and stretched. They had commandeered a conference room just down from the waiting room and had been at work for hours, putting the bits and pieces together.

"We're missing something," he said. "I wish I knew what."

A tap came to the door. Ben answered it, glanced at Caleb, and then took the note he was handed. He returned to the table and set it down in front of Caleb.

Caleb looked at it and then up at Ben.

"Hannah's at it again. You might as well read it and then fill us in." Ben's voice had that droll tone to it he had when he was trying not to laugh.

Caleb shook his head and then opened the note. Not again, he thought, not again. He handed the note to Ben and then Eddie. They nodded. Now it was all making sense. They just had to make sure they could follow the trail before it ran cold or the culprits had disappeared.

Another knock at the door, and Ben found Liam standing there. He pulled him in and waited. Caleb stood and faced his friend.

"We have word," Liam stated. "Leith is in recovery. There was some muscle damage and blood vessel damage but they are optimistic that he'll have a full recovery." Liam's voice broke and he staggered. Caleb caught his arm. "Regan is still in surgery. They haven't updated yet, but the last one was pretty grim. The bullet was really close to the heart."

Caleb placed his hand on his friend's shoulder in support. "God has not brought her through what they have gone through to let her die."

Eddie spoke up. "Caleb's right, Liam. Trust and pray."

Liam nodded and then slipped from the room.

Caleb looked at the two left. "Are we ready to roll? Plans are finalized. Can you think of anything we've missed?"

"No, just adding that name to our warrants search teams."

Eddie agreed. "We're ready. Let's go get them."

They gathered up their paperwork and headed back to organize and then execute the raids that were coming. They were winding it up and as far as Caleb was concerned, it was far too long.

****

Liam and Laycee stood by Leith's bed as he moved restlessly. The pain was evident in his face. Laycee's eyes sparkled with tears as she watched. It hurt to see Leith lying so white and in pain.

Liam's arm came around his sister and his other hand rested on his brother's arm. The surgeon has said it would be a while but he should be awake soon. They would wait, however long it took.

The surgeon had stopped on his way through and spoken with them. They trusted him and trusted God but it still hurt.

Regan's father stood as Regan's surgeon approached, a grim look on his face. They were expecting the worst. He sat beside them and searched for words. Rebecca's hand reached for her husband.

The surgeon hesitated and then spoke, "She came through surgery. It was not as bad as it seemed. The heart is fine; it wasn't touched. There's certainly damage in the area but we've done the best we can to repair it. Barring any bleeders or set backs, she'll be fine. We'll be monitoring her in Recovery for a while and then sending her to an ICU unit. I'll have a nurse come find you when we move her." He stopped, then looked at them again. "You do know that her heart stopped before she got here and the paramedics kept her alive. There were a couple of times in the operating room that I thought she was gone but she came back. I could tell that was when your prayers were the strongest."

Neither parent could speak but they nodded at him as he rose and walked away. Their daughter was alive, that's all that mattered. Caleb was looking after the rest.

Chapter 22

Caleb opened the door to the jewelry store and entered, officers coming in behind him and spreading out through the store. Adam Bell, the owner, approached him, an arrogant manner in his walk.

"What is this meaning of this, Chief? Why are you and your men here?" Adam Bell demanded.

Caleb said nothing, just wandered around the store, looking at the display cases. He wondered how many of these had been made with contraband jewels that cost next to nothing, if you didn't count lives lost.

"Well, I'm waiting. It's almost time to close and I have a meeting tonight for the Chamber of Commerce I have to be at in an hour." He pulled his sleeve back and uncovered the solid gold watch he was wearing.

Caleb took note of the jewelled rings on his hands and the jewelled tie pin. Still, he didn't answer, just kept wandering and taking note of the jewelry. As he reached the door where a curtain covered access to the back, he stopped and then motioned two officers through.

"How dare you, Chief Logan! That's a private staff are and workroom that no one is allowed into." The spit almost flew from Adam's mouth, he was so angry.

Caleb turned and made his way to stand three feet in front on him. Arms crossed on his chest, he continued to stare. He could see the sweat beading on Adam's face. Good, he thought. He's rattled. Keep it up, Caleb, he thought, and he'll make a slip.

Caleb continued to watch, not moving. He heard the officers return from the back and slanted his body slightly. At a nod from one, he turned back to Adam.

"That meeting is one you'll be missing, Adam."

"I don't think so. You and your men can leave."

"I don't think so, either, Adam because you see, you are under arrest."

"Under arrest? For what phony charges?"

Caleb stared him in the eye, then spoke, "Well, let's see. For starters, smuggling jewels. Then we'll add conspiracies for murder, intimidation, break-ins, theft, assault on police officers. I'm sure as we go along we will find more to add. And those are just our charges. The federal authorities are waiting to speak with you too."

"I'll have your badge and the badges of everyone in this room. I want to speak with my lawyer."

"Go ahead." Caleb turned away.

As Adam was being read his rights and handcuffed, Caleb turned back. "Just so you know, you won't be the only Bell in our jail tonight. Mark was arrested a couple of days ago and has been held in Oak City. That department is returning him to town tonight."

Adam howled and lunged at Caleb but was held firmly by the officers. They led him away, cursing and screaming vindictively.

Caleb looked around with sadness. Such a waste, he thought. So many years, so much pleasure Adam had given, all lost to greed.

Ben entered the store, and Caleb turned.

"I take it that didn't go over well."

"Not at all." Caleb sighed. "We'll have to let it work through the courts now. You and Eddie will be busy sorting everything out. You have a team with the warrant at his home?"

Ben nodded. "There are a lot of unhappy campers there, too. Eddie says he has tracked down a storage unit or two that Adam had in another name. We're getting warrants for them as well." Ben paused. "His wife works for the courts. She's the leak there. Hannah was right on again. Sure you can't put her on the payroll somehow?"

Caleb smiled at his friend's gentle teasing in the midst of the darkness. "We'll meet with the families in a few days. It will take a while to sort out all the whys and wherefores." Caleb paused and looked at out the evening sky. The sunset was brilliant in its pinks and reds and purples. "I'm going to head back to the hospital."

Ben laid a hand on Caleb's arm and stopped him. "You did well, Caleb. This has been a really hard case to crack. I don't think we could have solved it any sooner. Adam covered his tracks way too well."

Caleb nodded. "That's true, but there's little consolation in the fact that two young men are in jail as well as George and Adam, that two young men are dead, that we lost a really good secretary, and that two friends have ended up fighting more than once for their lives. I don't understand how God lets things like this happen. I can't doubt Him, but there are just times where I wonder."

"I know, Caleb. I'm the same. The only advice I can give is that God really does have a plan, that He knows the ending that will come. Trust is what it's all about."

Chapter 23

Ten days later, the group gathered in the Evans' home. Regan was ensconced on the couch, a quilt draped over her. She was still weak but being home was certainly making her feel better. She would never take home for granted again.

Leith sat beside her on the floor. His shoulder was still healing but he had already talked to Pietro, who had sent one of his grandsons to town to help. Paul loved the area and the work with Leith so much, the 22-year-old was doing his best to talk Leith into hiring him on a full-time basis. Regan and he had talked it over together and with Pietro. Paul would be staying.

The rest of the families had spread themselves out through the room. Eddie and Ben leaned against door frames, knowing what was coming, but relishing the re-telling of the story.

Caleb stood back to the fireplace and gazed around the room, eyes stopping on each one. Each one had been affected in some way or other. Some had been affected more. His glance stopped on Joseph and Rebecca, who had lost a business partner, brother, nephew, almost their reputation and more importantly their daughter. Regan was next. She had her head bent talking with Leith. Those two, he thought, yes those two. They have had an adventure of a life time but had learned so much of God's care. Regan called Leith her Hawk, who watched for game. He had provided for her in so many ways over this hard days. Caleb brought to the mind the verse speaking of the hawk and thought how true it was when Caleb headed them south to town.

Liam was next. He stood alone yet strong. He was the eldest, the protector of the family. What name would suit him best, Caleb wondered? Somewhere someone would find one that just fit him. He had been through a lot with his two siblings in the last six or seven months. He needed a break.

Laycee sat curled up in an easy chair, feet tucked up under her. The sparrow,

Caleb thought of her. Little but noisy; noisy but so important to the family. She had been through so much a few months ago. As had his brother, Joshua, who perched on the arm of her chair. He was so thankful everything had worked out for him last year and that he was here today.

Caleb cleared his throat and all eyes fell on him. Where to start he wondered?

"It's hard to know exactly where to start. I guess with George. George was the contact who would find the uncut stones, steal them and then secret them in the cases of tiles. They had been doing this likely for 10 years or so from what he says. He was also one of the Knights as Adam Bell called them.

"Next is David Sullivan. He was called the Innocent. He provided access for George to the store to retrieve the stolen gems.

"Eric Brand was the Jester as he was called. He pretty much was a gopher, working between Adam, David and anyone they hired to do some dirty work. This kept Adam's name and face out of it. I don't think Eric knew who he was working for.

"Mark Bell was really just a courier. He had no idea what his father was up to. He was asked to deliver packets of gems at times and had no idea that they were stolen.

"Susan, our secretary. That's a hard pill to swallow. She had been married to Eric, divorced, and took back her maiden name. Their marriage had been out of the area and didn't show up on her initial check. The check has now been improved.

"Jane Bell, Adam's wife. She worked at the court house and helped to hide information on background checks.

"Adam Bell. Our town jeweller. The one we turned to for so many years for so many jewelry items. We will never know if we have a stolen gem or not. He set himself up as the King of an empire and basically thumbed his nose at us.

"We do know that George is responsible for the murder of Eric. Eric murdered David. Mark was set up to come ask for information by his father, which backfired on them. I doubt he knew exactly why Adam wanted that. George is responsible for the kidnappings. We are still tracking the other Knight but our suspicion is that George took care of him.

"Now I think that's it. It all stemmed around greed and lust for money. Adam had planned in the next couple of years to wind down his store and retire, supposedly to the south but he had bank accounts overseas and was really planning on a name change and a country change."

They sat absorbing Caleb's words.

Ben spoke. "It is ironic, Leith. The Bell House you worked on—it was Adam's grandparents before it was sold. He never forgave his parents for selling it. Part of the vindictiveness directed to you is from that, that you changed how it looked from what he remembered to what the new owner asked for."

Regan hesitated, then spoke. "I have known for years that David was no good. He was always cruel." She looked at her parents with tears in her eyes. "I had to leave. I couldn't stand to be around him. He had threatened friends and hinted at causing you harm. I should have spoken up but I was just so scared."

Her parents were shocked. They knew the two younger people had not gotten on but hadn't realized it was to this extent. This would take time to absorb.

"What about John?" Liam asked. "Was his a natural death?"

"As far as we can determine it was. If there were factors leading up to it, they were not physical. We will never know if he found out about David or not."

Joseph spoke up. "He knew. We had talked. He was trying to find a program that he could get David into but he ran out of time."

They had a lot to absorb and a lot of healing to do.

"Why don't we gather back here in a day or two?" Rebecca asked. "You too, Eddie and Ben, and your wives. Hannah and the boys, too. We'll have had some time to think and if we have more questions, maybe we'll have answers then."

Leith waited for the room to clear, then stood and gathered Regan into his arms and sat back down. She looked at him.

"You're taking a lot of liberty, boy."

Leith laughed. "No, just an armful of woman." He tilted his head to look at her. "How are you really doing?"

"I hurt in ways I never imagined I could, but with God I will get through it." She looked at him. "Now put me down. You need to go home."

He laughed again, dropped a quick kiss on her surprised mouth and then left.

Epilogue

Three months had passed. Leith and Regan had healed physically but they were still working through some issues.

Regan sat on a wicker chair on her apartment deck. She had finally made the move to her own place, content to be back in her home town. Her place overlooked a large park and the river and she loved it.

She heard the door open behind her and knew Leith had come out. A mug of coffee appeared in front of her nose.

"You're taking a lot for granted, aren't you, buster?" She laughed.

"That I am." He leaned in for a quick kiss, then pulled up the wicker chair beside her. They sat in silence watching the sky and the river.

"Leith, I can't tell you how grateful I am for your care over the last few months. When we were going through that awful, awful time, you were there, even hurt, to watch out."

Leith shrugged. "I care very deeply about you." He turned to study her. "We need to do another day away."

"Oh no," Regan stated as he laughed, shaking her head. "One of those days away is enough."

"This time, my darling, it will be different. You're not in danger any more. Life is more sane." He reached for her hand. "Laycee had the right idea. She asked Joshua to go steady. Will you be my girl?"

Regan's head tipped and she studied him. "Well…." He wrapped his hand around her neck, drew her forward and kissed her. "Okay, steady as she goes they say."

He leaned his head on hers and laughed. "I can see a sea voyage in our future. As long as we have the Captain we need, we're set."

Regan's hand touched his face. "Yes, my Hawk. Our Captain never fails."

A noise interrupted them. "What is that?" Leith asked.

Regan giggled and reached down beside her. "Close your eyes." When he had, she handed him a puppy.

Wriggling, the puppy reached to lick Leith's face. His eyes popped open and he laughed. Petting the puppy and trying to get it to lay still, he had to ask. "What kind of dog is this? I don't think I've seen that colouring before."

"I talked to Laycee who had a friend whose Sheltie had had pups. This is what you call a bi-blue. It's the gray, white, black combination." She reached to stroke the puppy's back. "You get to name her."

"A dog, hmm." Leith sat back cradling the puppy. "A girl. Well, I think Abby would be a good name for her."

"That didn't take long," Regan laughed. "I think that's a good name. Now," as she reached down again, "what do we call our calico kitten?" as a kitten made its appearance.

Leith shouted with laughter, startling the two animals. "That name, my darling, is up to you."

"Well, then, I guess she'll be Emmy."

Leith leaned over and kissed the woman he loved. "You, my darling, have made my life complete. We will definitely have a wonderful adventure together."

Regan was silent for a few months, then spoke. "When we were going through all that and I didn't think we would make it through, God really emphasized how He had provided the strong tower for us to run to, to protect us. In some ways, it felt like He hadn't but I know He did. I never want to forget that."

Leith's hand caught her free hand in a strong grip. "We never will, my darling. We never will. He will never let us."

Dear Readers:

Thank you so much for joining me in the next book for the Bradley Family, the story of the youngest, Leith.

Once again, a Bradley sibling is in danger and has to rely on others but more importantly on God. Twists and turns once more dominate. I love a good story where you can't figure out whodunnit until the end and I have tried so hard to incorporate that in the stories.

The story of Laycee was a dream novel - a dream novel in the sense that I have always wanted to put pen to paper, or in modern terms, fingers to keyboard, and create a story. That dream was the last one I shared with my Mother.

In this story, I have tried so hard to show that God is our strong tower. When we need comfort, a place to rest, a place to hide from whatever is betting us, He is that strong tower for us. I have a picture in my mind (and each of us will have a different picture) of a high rough stone building, with some small windows, stone work around the top with openings for weapons and lines of sight, but more importantly, only one door.

One door to enter, we don't need more than one.

The story of Leith incorporates my heritage. The name Bradley was given to my Dad by his parents. It was my Grandmother's maiden name. I have teaspoons engraved with the stylized B that she brought from England with her back in 1919. My Dad was a carpenter and worked in that trade until he was 74. He had had to learn more than just wood — he laid foundations, laid blockwork, did drywall, plaster, tiles. The words Leith speaks to Regan about how hard construction is on a woman and the atmosphere that is quite often found on a job site—those were my Dad's to me. I wanted so much to enter a trade. He felt I needed to do other. But that's okay. His example and teaching have lead me to remodel my own house with my own hands, from installing plumbing fixtures to tiling to laying laminate flooring and anything I could find to do inbetween. The very first task I did was to install a new back door, which Dad and I had debated over whether it would fit or not. It fit. He would come up and ask if I had done something, tell me what to do, and then step back.   His words when I finished are treasures: You did a wonderful job.   He graduated to heaven in 2012 but I know I would be hearing that today if he were here.

So my friends, I don't know what you are facing in your lives right now.   None of us know the plans or the plots or the twists and turns that God allows in our lives.   He is the Author of Life and knows the ways and means of where He is leading us.   Never be afraid to say to Him you don't understand, that you need comfort.   Run to the Strong Tower that He is.

Ronna